ROMANCING *the* RANGER

A COTTON CREEK ROMANCE

JENNIE MARTS

Entangled Publishing, LLC
2614 South Timberline Road
Suite 109
Fort Collins, CO 80525
Visit our website at www.entangledpublishing.com.

Lovestruck is an imprint of Entangled Publishing, LLC.

Edited by Allison Collins
Cover design by Heather Howland
Cover art from Shutterstock

Manufactured in the United States of America

First Edition March 2016

This book is for Todd—
My favorite park ranger
And the one who taught me everything I know about
romance

Chapter One

Reese Hudson knew she was driving too fast. She didn't care. She wanted to put as much distance between herself and the smug jerk she'd actually been considering marrying.

What had she been thinking?

The Lexus hugged the Colorado mountain road as it rounded another curve. The scent of pine filled the car as she cracked her window and breathed in the warm summer air.

A cardboard box full of mementos of the life she no longer wanted sat in the passenger seat. A life full of emptiness and control. Destroying the box and its pitifully small contents was the first step to breaking free.

She rounded another curve, and the box slid into the ample rump of the fat pug that shared the seat. The dog grunted his annoyance.

"Sorry, Bagel." She let up on the gas and breathed a sigh of relief as she passed the green sign reading, COTTON CREEK FALLS—3 MILES. Her special place. Her grandparents had been bringing her to the waterfall near their small town of Cotton Creek since she was old enough to walk.

Her phone buzzed, and the display on the dashboard read "Robert Hudson—CEO of Hudson Holdings." Releasing a different kind of sigh, she steeled herself for the conversation. "Hi, Dad."

"Reese. Are you okay?" Her father's booming voice filled the car, and Bagel produced a whine followed by exuberant tail-wagging.

"Hello, Bagel." Her father's greeting to the dog held more affection than his greeting to her.

She waited for the scolding to begin.

"What's going on? I heard you left the office early today?" *Of course he did.*

She was sure he'd been flooded with reports of her dramatic exit by butt-kissing employees who wanted to get in good with the boss by keeping tabs on his daughter. "Yes, I did."

Short and to the point. Just the kind of answers her dad, and her boss, liked.

"I also heard you and Brock are having a little trouble?"

"Really? A little trouble, Dad? A little trouble is running out of paper towels in the ladies' room. Brock and I are done. We've been dating almost a year, and he still can't spell my name right. He thinks it makes more sense to spell it with a *C*."

And if it made sense to Brock, then it must be so. He was a man used to getting his own way, controlling everything in his environment. Just like the man she spoke with on the phone.

No wonder they got along so well. Brock was a mini-me of her father.

"Well, I'm sure you two will work it out. Brock seems like too good a catch to throw away over a simple spelling error. You know you're closing in on thirty, and your options may start to diminish before long."

Wow. Her dad always knew what to say to comfort her.

"In the meantime, we've still got a business to run, Reese. I thought you had an appointment with the Donaldsons today."

"I rescheduled. They were fine with it." The older couple were her favorite customers and one of the few things she liked about her job as a financial advisor. She loathed crunching numbers and talking interest rates but she liked helping people. People like the Donaldsons.

"Where are you?"

"I'm going for a drive."

"You're headed up to that damn waterfall, aren't you?"

"Yes, Dad. It makes me happy, and I need a dose of happiness right now."

She heard him sigh and imagined him running his hand through his still dark hair. "Your mother loved it there, too."

The tone of his voice softened her. Just like it always did when he spoke of her mother. She knew losing his wife at such a young age had changed him and made him overprotective of his only child.

Which is why she forgave him. Again. And again.

"Gotta go, Dad. I'll call you later." She disconnected the call as she turned into the overlook.

Scanning the empty parking lot, she pulled into a space near an old picnic table. A dilapidated outhouse sat nearby, the path to the falls overlook on its right.

Rolling down the windows for the dog, she caught the faint sound of rushing water and a feeling of peace washed over her. It lasted about three seconds—replaced with frustration as she opened the door and snagged her hose getting out.

Stupid panty hose. Nobody even wore them anymore.

Nobody except old ladies and apparently Brock's girlfriend. One more example of the ridiculous things she put herself through to please him.

She reached her fingers into the snag and ripped a giant hole in the silky material.

Ha—take that, you panty-hose-loving control freak.

Grabbing the file box, she carried it to the picnic table, heels sinking into the gravel parking lot as she walked. The warm summer air eased her soul, and she unbuttoned her suit jacket and took a deep breath before facing the carton of memories.

What a pathetic collection of keepsakes. The relics of their relationship didn't even fill the box: a few pictures, a book, an expensive desk set, and a bottle of scotch.

Who gives a woman a bottle of scotch as a gift?

She dug through the assorted papers and held up an invitation to the Spring Ball, one they'd attended a few weeks ago.

The one where Brock had coolly informed the waiter that she would pass on dessert then informed her that he'd noticed her dress was a little snug in the hips and suggested she up her cardio time at the gym.

She looked around for a trash can, ready to dispose of not just the man, but every memory she had of him. When she'd first met him, he'd won her over with his good looks and charm. They seemed a perfect fit.

Goes to show you can't judge a book by its cover. His gorgeous cover hid the fact that his book was full of conceit and smug vanity and titled *101 Ways to Be an Asshole*.

Reese vowed that her days of dating country club jackasses were over. The next man she went out with would be the opposite of Brock.

He wouldn't care about what kind of car he drove and wouldn't have to match his sock color to his tie. A man who wouldn't worry about dog hair on his suit pants.

Hell, he was out if he even wore a suit.

She wanted a guy who wore jeans and knew how to relax. Who could enjoy a slice of pizza without figuring out the nutritional value and calculating the number of squats he would need to do to burn off that bite's calories.

So basically someone she could like. And her dad would hate.

She tore the invitation in half.

It wasn't enough.

She needed to purge herself of this man's energy. She spied a lighter lying in the box, part of the desk set Brock had given her for her birthday this year. The lavish and expensive desk set was probably the nicest one his secretary could find.

Who needed jewelry or flowers when she could have a gold-plated letter opener with a matching notepad?

She picked up the lighter and flicked the handle, the gold flame licking the corner of the invitation, until the heavy paper finally caught fire.

The flame quickly flared and burned the tips of her fingers.

"Holy shit—ouch!"

Dropping the note, she pulled the scorched tips to her mouth. The box sat on the edge of the table, and her arm bumped the corner and knocked it to the ground.

The sound of glass shattering told her the bottle of scotch had broken in the fall.

• • •

Ranger Wade Baker took the familiar turns of the mountain road with ease. His phone was tucked between his ear and his shoulder as he listened to his grandmother's request.

"I just need one thing from the store, honey," Miss Abigail was saying, "I went grocery shopping yesterday but forgot to get a pair of panty hose, and I need them for the church supper tonight."

He rolled his eyes. "All right Gram, I guess I can buy you a pair of panty hose. Can you give me one other thing we need so it's not my only purchase?"

"Oh sure, why don't you grab me a bottle of clear nail polish, in case I get a run."

He laughed. "Yeah, panty hose and nail polish. That'll make my holdings in man-stock go right up."

"All right, I don't want anyone revoking your man-card. We can always use another loaf of bread. Is that a more macho purchase? Just make sure the panty hose are suntan-colored and size queen in a tall."

"Nice. You know, if I walk into the grocery asking for tall-sized pantyhose, the clerk is going to think I've started dressing in drag."

Wade considered his petite five-foot-nothing grandmother. "Besides that Gram, why in the world would you need queen-size or tall anything?"

"The queen-size ones are so much easier to put on, and I can pull up the talls so the crotch doesn't stop at my knees. The ones they make for my size are so small and tight that they take a forklift and a bottle of lube to squeeze into." She giggled at her own joke.

Wade chuckled at the sound of his grandmother's laughter. She'd raised him for most of his life, and he was used to her somewhat off-color humor. "Gram, I'll get the panty hose, just please don't ever say 'lube' to me again. In any capacity."

She giggled harder, let out a tiny snort, and he was afraid she was going to choke. "I'm driving up to the falls to eat my lunch. Text me if you think of anything else you might need."

His grandmother caught her breath. "That should be it. Did you see I packed you a sandwich with that good meatloaf from last night?"

Even though he was a full-grown man, Miss Abigail still considered it her duty to pack his lunch every day. "I'm looking forward to it. You know how I love your meatloaf, Gram."

Her laughter died as she brought up the next topic. "I got

the mail today, and there was another bill from the credit card company. Just gets my dander up every time I see those. I'm sorry, honey, but that woman should be in jail. She was a real piece of work. I know you cared about her, but you really dodged a bullet getting away from that one."

He may have dodged the bullet, but just barely. He'd had the gun cocked and loaded, given her the engagement ring and set the date.

He'd spent the last year of his life in a roller coaster of emotions and ended up being swindled by a gorgeous woman who made him feel both as big as life and as poor as a church mouse.

He'd thought he loved her, but Tawnya Rollins had played him like a fine-tuned fiddle.

She'd sucked him in, made him believe she loved him. But as soon as she got the engagement ring on her finger, she'd started to change.

For every word she used to build his confidence, she had another to tear him down. One minute he was the master of the universe, the next an inconvenient pebble in her shoe.

Nothing he did seemed to ever be enough.

He didn't take her out enough, he didn't compliment her enough, and he didn't make enough money to buy her the kinds of gifts she thought she deserved. She took his self-esteem everywhere except in the bedroom, where she lavished on the attention and made him feel like a king.

She had his heart so twisted and his mind so muddled, he didn't know which way was up.

They'd decided on a Christmas wedding, and she loved making all the plans. She was never happier than when she was buying things or reserving stuff for the big day.

She'd convinced him to open a joint credit card "just for wedding stuff" and then another at a department store where she "just had to get a few things for the honeymoon."

Unfortunately he hadn't paid as much attention as he should have, until he came home early one day and picked up the mail before she did.

Amongst the normal junk and advertising flyers, he found statements for the credit cards and realized they'd both been maxed out. He'd scanned the statements and couldn't believe the sheer number of purchases Tawnya had made.

He was stunned at the thousands of dollars tallied up for designer clothes, shoes, expensive purses and jewelry. Who knew you could spend that much on cosmetics and underwear?

He'd broken it off that night, and she'd left him with a colossal pile of debt and the parting words that if only he had a real job that made decent money, he would have been able to provide for her, and this never would have happened.

Nursing a wounded heart and a damaged ego, he researched his options and realized there was nothing he could do. The cards were in his name as well, so he was equally responsible for the debt.

His life was now a constant battle fighting the credit bureaus and department stores, and trying to salvage his pride and his credit by keeping up on the monthly payments and slowly paying off the debt. Because that's what Baker men did, they took care of their obligations, whether they'd created them or not.

Thoughts of interest rates and debt consolidation filled his head as he pulled into the parking lot of the falls and spied the Lexus.

On a normal day, he would have been happy to share his lunch break with an attractive curvy blonde, but today all he noticed were her nice clothes and expensive haircut, and he saw red.

It took him a minute to realize she was burning something. "I gotta go, Gram, I've got a situation." He hung up the phone and gawked at the woman.

What the hell did she think she was doing? Fires weren't allowed here. There was a fire ban in place.

. . .

The sound of an engine startled Reese, and she looked up as a green Park Service truck pulled into the parking lot.

"What the hell are you doing?" the park ranger asked, stepping out of the truck.

Reese registered blue jeans and cowboy boots on a tall, muscular frame. The man's sandy blond hair held the natural highlights she paid dearly to achieve every month at the salon.

He wore a brown uniform shirt and a scowl on his otherwise handsome face.

A *whoosh* of flames burst at her feet. She jumped back as the fire spread to the tall dry grass in front of the outhouse.

Oh no! What have I done?

Panic welled in her chest as she pulled off her suit jacket and whacked the ground, trying to stamp out the fire.

As if it had a mind of its own, the flames headed straight for the dry timber of the outhouse, searching for more fuel to sate its fiery hunger.

Focused on the fire, she didn't look up, but heard the ranger swear and radio for help. Then he ran up beside her, a fire extinguisher in his hands as she vehemently tried to put out the flames.

"Get back," he yelled.

Her dog barked feverishly in the car. She wasn't sure if it was at the fire or the man wielding the big red canister.

A glance at the car showed the dog scrambling out the open window, his yapping replaced with a painful yelp as he fell to the ground.

"Bagel!" she cried as the injured dog limped toward her.

She ran for the dog, oblivious of the ranger wielding the extinguisher. Intent on getting to Bagel, she ran right in front of him.

"Aahh!" she cried as a shot of white foam hit her in the chest. Shocked, she stumbled, her heel broke, and she fell to the ground. The little dog whined as it limped to her.

"Come here, baby." She pulled it into her arms, cradling its hurt leg while trying to keep it from licking the white foam from her bare arms.

"Are you okay?" the ranger called to her as he continued to fight the flames that now engulfed half of the park's outhouse.

The sound of a siren filled the air, and another Park Service vehicle arrived, equipped with a water tank and hose. Two men jumped from the truck and had the fire extinguished within a few minutes.

One of the men patted the ranger on the back. "You all right, Wade? Lucky for you, we were already coming up the pass when we heard your call."

Wade ignored the fireman and turned to her, his face full of anger. "What the hell were you thinking? You could have set the whole forest on fire. This is a state park, and we're under a fire ban."

"I'm sorry. I didn't mean to." She awkwardly tried to stand, wobbling on one foot with the hurt dog in her arms, her broken shoe lost somewhere in the chaos of the fire.

A low chuckle sounded from one of the firefighting rangers as he glanced at her chest.

She looked down to see the liquid from the extinguisher had turned her ivory camisole see-through. The white lace bra she wore was no help in concealing her assets, and her headlights took advantage of that moment to shine.

That's just great.

She lifted the dog higher as Wade stripped off his shirt

and held it out to her. Distracted by his broad shoulders and seriously muscled chest, she clumsily handed him the dog and took the shirt. Tearing her eyes from his slim tapered waist and tanned bare skin, she pulled the warm shirt around her. It smelled like aftershave and campfire smoke. "Thanks. Look, I really am sorry. I'm happy to pay for the damages."

She felt horrible for starting the fire. Her stomach ached at the thought of what could have happened.

But her regret was lost on the ranger.

His face darkened with anger. That had apparently been the wrong thing to say. "What's wrong with you people from the city? You think you can come up here with your fancy clothes and your flashy cars and disregard all the rules. You could have caused some real damage here. You don't care about anyone but yourselves. Money doesn't fix everything, lady."

Whoa. This guy was hot. And not just in a handsome way. In a seriously pissed off way.

She needed to tread lighter. Not make him any angrier.

Hmmm. Why did this feel familiar?

Because this was what she always did. With her father. With Brock.

Hadn't the purpose of her drive up here been to take back control of her life? To throw away not just the mementos but the bad habits of trying to please everyone else and bending over backward to not get anyone upset?

The only way to quit being weak was to be assertive.

No time like the present.

She squared her shoulders and stared the ranger in the eye. "Look, mister. It was an accident. I said I was sorry and offered to pay for the damages. That's my offer. What are you going to do about it?"

Thirty minutes later, she was reconsidering her decision to test her newfound assertiveness on Ranger Wade as she cooled her one dusty heel in a jail cell.

Chapter Two

She would not cry. Damn it.

It was just a jail cell.

Reese took a deep breath and focused on the positives. She had the whole cell to herself, so that was good. No sharing with a creepy ax murderer. The quiet would allow her to use the time to contemplate how she'd gotten here and how she was going to get *out* of here.

The two jail cells were located in the back of the police station that Ranger Wade had marched her into several hours ago.

They must have looked quite a sight to the shocked dispatcher and two police officers sitting at their desks. Wade shirtless and carrying a fat sausage of a dog and her limping along with only one shoe and wearing his shirt.

Both were smudged with soot, and chunks of her hair had hardened where the extinguisher foam had landed and dried.

A rotund police officer had taken Wade's statement and left her in this cell with nothing but a pompous look and her wounded pride.

Who knew what they'd done with Bagel?

She'd yelled herself silly for the first half hour, but when no one came to her aid, she'd sunk down onto the cot in defeat.

The ginormous hole in her hose stared up at her as if it were an eye and suddenly the fabric of the stockings seemed to bind and tighten, suffocating her lower half.

She hated everything about these stupid hose. From their sheer toe to their control top. Even the name of them had control in it.

She stood and turned, leaning on the cot for support as she hiked up her skirt and pulled the offensive material from her legs.

Freeing one leg, she let out a sigh and her constricted stomach muscles at the same time.

Ahh. Freedom at last.

She peeled the hose from her other leg.

"What in the hell are you doing?"

Reese shrieked as the deep male voice spoke from behind her, and she frantically reached to pull her skirt back down over her exposed bottom.

She hadn't quite freed her foot from the hose and the motion countered her balance. She toppled over, grazing her head on the corner of the cot as she fell.

Pain seared through her forehead, and shame filled her cheeks as she crumpled to the floor, burying her face in her arms, the tears she'd been holding in finally ready to fall.

The sound of keys jangled, then the door screeched open.

The scurrying tap of tiny toenails against concrete preceded the thud of Bagel's chubby body as he plowed into her in a frenzied panic to lick her face.

She sat up, cuddling the dog in her lap. His back leg was wrapped in a white bandage, and a drop of bright red blood fell onto the gauze as she leaned forward to check the dog's foot.

"You're not really having the best day there, are ya lady?" Ranger Wade bent before her, a paper towel in his hand. He'd washed up and wore a fresh uniform shirt.

She groaned inwardly at what a disaster she must look like. "You don't know the half of it. And my name is Reese. Reese Hudson."

He tipped up her head and dabbed at the cut on her forehead. "Reese? Like the peanut butter cup?"

"Yep. Only singular." She tried to nod, but winced at the pain. "It seems like you're quite the hero today. Putting out the fire and now offering first aid. Did you bandage my dog's leg, too?"

"No. I took him over to my vet to get him checked out. I was worried he broke his dang leg falling out of the car like that. But Doc said it's only a sprain. He needs to rest and not be too active."

She arched an eyebrow at the ranger. "Does this dog look like it's ever been *too* active?"

That earned her a grin, but before he could answer, a young police officer poked his head in the cell. "The judge is ready for her."

"A judge? Already?" Her pulse quickened.

She'd never been in trouble before, and the idea of going into a courtroom to face a judge scared the hell out of her.

The officer nodded. "We don't have a lot of court cases here in Cotton Creek Falls. Plus it's Friday afternoon, so the judge wants to clear this case from the docket so he can go fishing this weekend."

"What about my one phone call? Or getting a lawyer?"

"Do you want one of those?"

Did she want one of those? Who would she even call? Certainly not her dad.

And even though the company had several lawyers on retainer, there was no way she was calling one of them. She didn't need this getting back to her dad.

Or to Brock.

Besides, waiting for a lawyer would mean more time spent in this cell, possibly the entire weekend. *No thank you.*

She wanted to take control, stand on her own two feet. Now was her chance.

She could certainly handle defending herself in a small-town court. The fire was an accident. It hadn't been malicious. All she had to do was explain that to the judge.

She shook her head. "No, I'll take care of this myself."

"Let's go, then." The officer opened the cell door and cringed at her bloody forehead. "Looks like you're gonna need a Band-Aid."

• • •

"The honorable Judge T. Booker presiding. You may be seated."

Wade sat behind the small plaintiff's table as the bailiff instructed. He'd known the judge since before he could walk and wasn't concerned about him not meting out a fair judgment.

This was a small-town court, though, and the judge was also known for handing down unconventional solutions for some of the townsfolk's lesser crimes.

He couldn't believe how fast that fire had sparked, and he cringed at the harm it could have done. The other rangers had shown up just in time, and he was thankful the fire hadn't spread and caused any worse damage.

He knew it was probably an accident, but damn it, this park meant something to him, and he'd yelled at her before he could stop himself.

In retrospect, he'd probably let his temper get the best of him. She had seemed sorry, standing there in her smoke-smudged clothes with a giant hole in her snagged-up panty hose. And her top covered in liquid foam.

Hello. That fire extinguisher was supposed to put out flames, but what it did to her flimsy little shirt had worked to ignite some new ones.

Looking embarrassed, she'd taken his shirt, and he'd softened a little when she'd passed him the hurt dog.

The fat little thing licked his chin, and he was this close to letting the whole thing go.

Then she had to go throwing her pocketbook around, acting like money was the answer to everything. Well, he had news for this lady. All her money wasn't going to get her out of this mess.

He snuck a glance at Reese now. She sat at the table across from him, and despite the circumstances, he couldn't deny she was still attractive. Hell, she was gorgeous. Long blond hair, green eyes, legs a mile long, curvy hips, and pouty red lips—the kind of woman men had fantasies about.

Although, she currently looked pretty pathetic wearing only one shoe and swallowed up in his soot-stained uniform shirt. Drops of blood from her cut were already drying on the sleeve to a dull brown color.

Someone had brought her a white gauze bandage for her forehead, and she and the dog were a matched set with their medical accessories.

His face warmed as he thought about the image he'd walked in on thirty minutes earlier. Reese bent over the side of the cot, her skirt hiked up, and her bare cheeks visible around the tiny white lace thong.

Holy hell. His mouth went dry, and his hands started to sweat at the same time.

Her figure was perfect. Just the way he liked it, curvy and lush. He loved the feel of a soft voluptuous woman in his arms, with a body he could grab onto and fill his hands with.

Whoa there, bucko. Who said anything about filling his hands with anything of Reese Hudson's?

This woman spelled trouble with a capital *T*. It didn't matter how sweet her cheeks were, he wanted nothing to do with this poor little rich girl.

The judge cleared his throat and looked up from the file. "It says here on your license that your name is Reese O'Neal Hudson. Any relation to Bud and Dorothy O'Neal?"

Reese nodded. "They were my grandparents. I used to come up here to visit them when I was a kid. I love Cotton Creek Falls. It's one of my favorite places. I would never purposely try to destroy it. I've already offered to pay for the damages."

All the sympathy Wade had been feeling drained away as she turned to money as the answer to the problem. "This isn't like a speeding ticket where you pay the fine and move on. Somebody's going to have to go up there and clean up the mess you left behind. It's going to take the state's resources and manpower to replace that building. And we don't have a lot of either to spare."

The judge held up a hand. "All right now. Simmer down there, son. I'm sure we can come up with a solution that will be reasonable to all the parties involved." He looked thoughtfully between Wade and Reese as he tapped his desk with his index finger.

Picking up his pen, the judge made some notes in the file, cleared his throat, and addressed Reese. "Ms. Hudson, your grandpa and I were fishing buddies since before you were born, so I'm prepared to offer you a little leniency. However, Ranger Baker does have a point in that the outbuilding will need to be replaced. Therefore I am sentencing you to two weeks community service whereby *you* will be responsible for rebuilding the restroom at the falls."

"That sounds fine," she said. "Can you recommend a

construction company or just tell me who to write the check out to?"

The judge chuckled. "There won't be any construction company. The sentence is for *you* to build it yourself."

Reese gaped at the judge, her mouth opening and closing like a trout on a hook. "But…but…I have no idea how to build an outhouse. I wouldn't even know where to start."

"That is precisely the point. If I gave you an easy task, it wouldn't be much of a punishment. This way you can make restitution for the damage to the property and repair what you destroyed. If you're determined to write a check, it probably wouldn't hurt if you made a nice donation to the park as well." The judge turned to Wade. "And before that smug grin takes over your entire face, Ranger Baker, I'm putting you in charge of supervising her work."

"Me? Why me? I didn't do anything." This wasn't turning out at all like he'd hoped. "You've got to be kidding, Judge."

The judge fixed him with a hard stare. "Do I look like I'm kidding?"

"But I don't have time for this. I have a job to do." He didn't have time to babysit this little rich chick who probably didn't know a hammer from a screwdriver.

Well, she was about to learn. He'd be damned if he ended up doing all the work while she sat around and painted her nails. She probably didn't even paint her own nails.

The judge banged his gavel. "You've heard my ruling. My decision is final. Ms. Hudson, you'll be required to stay in town for the next two weeks."

"Two weeks? But I have a job, too. A life." She slumped in her seat.

The judge arched an eyebrow at Wade. "I won't require her to stay in the county jail if Ranger Baker is willing to accept guardianship. Wade, I'm sure your grandmother has room for her over at the bed and breakfast. Why don't you take Ms. Hudson over there now? She looks like she could use a rest. I'll have someone drop her car over there later this evening. Are you amenable to that, Ms. Hudson, or do you prefer the fine accommodations of county lockup?"

She offered the judge a glazed nod. "A bed and breakfast sounds great." She lifted a hand to her bandaged head. "In fact, any bed sounds great right about now. Thank you, Judge."

Well, this was a fine kettle of fish. Wade had wanted to be rid of this pampered princess, not sentenced to spend the next two weeks with her. And now she'd be staying at Gram's place so he'd be stuck with her at night, too.

At least she was easy on the eyes. Or would be, if she cleaned up a little. Maybe this wouldn't be so bad. He'd get to kick back and spend the next few weeks watching a beautiful woman do manual labor, bending and stretching as she hammered and cut lumber.

He'd bet Ms. Reese Hudson could wear the hell out of a tool belt.

Yeah, right. Ms. Hudson did not strike him as the type of woman who got her pretty little hands dirty.

She only had one shoe left, but even he knew it was an expensive style. He recognized the name on her purse as one Tawnya constantly coveted, and bet the price tag on the purse alone could pay off one of those damn credit card statements that filled the stack on his desk at home.

He grimaced as he snuck a glance at Reese.

She held the dog against her, its plump body covering her lap as she stroked its fur and it nibbled her hand.

He knew the next two weeks with Reese Hudson were going to try all of his patience, but danged if he didn't feel a tiny stab of envy for the dog as he imagined Reese stroking his back while he found a few places of hers to nibble.

Chapter Three

What a mess she'd gotten herself into.

She'd set out this afternoon on a quest to express her freedom and gain control of her life. Instead she'd landed herself in jail and under the thumb of another man who would spend the next two weeks telling her what to do.

As far as men were concerned, if she had to be chained to one, Wade Baker wasn't the worst choice she could think of. He did have some redeeming qualities.

Even when his face wore a frown of annoyance, he was still a gentleman.

She could tell he was angry, yet his hand was gentle as they left the courthouse and he helped her into the passenger side of an old pickup truck.

He drove down Main Street then pulled into the Cotton Creek Drug Emporium, the small-town equivalent of a Walmart. "You're probably gonna need a few things. It's not fancy, but they've got toothpaste and most of your essentials. I'll wait with Bagel if you want to run in." He casually leaned back in the seat as if he didn't have a care in the world.

Wow. This was new.

Brock always hated when she had to run into a store, even if it was for a bottle of wine to take to a party of *his* friends. He'd explained that his time was valuable, and she needed to complete errands *before* he picked her up.

"Thanks," she said, climbing from the truck. "Would you like for me to get anything for you?"

He let out a whoosh of breath. "Oh yeah. I almost forgot. I need a pair of panty hose. Suntan-colored, in queen-size talls."

She arched an eyebrow at him. Maybe there was more to the ranger than she'd first imagined.

He rolled his eyes. "They're for my grandma. She asked me to pick some up for her for the church supper tonight."

She nodded. "Suntan. Queen-size. Talls. Got it."

As casual as Wade seemed, the image of his scowl stuck in her head, and Reese made a quick run around the drugstore grabbing a bag of dog food, assorted toiletries, a couple pairs of shorts, a few T-shirts, some flip-flops, a pair of canvas tennis shoes, and a value pack of bikini underwear. She hadn't bought underwear in a package since she was a child.

She found the requested panty hose and added them to her stack.

On a whim, she dropped a package of snack cupcakes on the pile and grabbed a couple of candy bars. Her stomach growled, and she realized she hadn't eaten since breakfast.

The look of surprise on Wade's face as she tossed him one of the candy bars didn't compare to the disbelief she'd experienced when she opened the truck door to see her chubby little dog curled in his lap, contentedly getting his chin scratched.

Brock wouldn't even let the dog into his car, let alone stoop to actually pet the creature.

Wade unwrapped the candy bar and actually smiled at her before he caught himself and returned to his usual scowl.

That small smile gave her stomach a tiny flip. She liked the way one side of his mouth tipped up.

"Here you go." She passed him the plastic sleeve containing the hose.

"Thanks." He handed her a five dollar bill.

Waving it away, she said, "No, it's fine. I've got it."

"I don't need you to pay for my…" He paused. "Panty hose. Well, my grandmother's panty hose." His scowl deepened as she tried not to laugh. "Just take the money."

She held up her hands in surrender and stuffed the bill into her purse. "Okay, I'll take the money."

The scenery of the town passed by in a blur, and Reese tried to draw him out of his shell. Anything to earn a glimpse of that gorgeous smile once more.

Thinking men liked to talk about their trucks, she went for a completely passive topic of conversation. "I like your truck."

Instead of the side-tipped grin, he frowned and practically growled an answer at her. "Yeah, sorry. My Mercedes is in the shop."

Okay, that didn't work. She tried a different topic. "So how long have you lived with your grandma?"

"She took me in when I was a kid after my mom decided the small-town life wasn't for her. She liked things that were new and sparkly, and my shine must have worn off. My dad followed her, and my grandma took me in. After college, I came back and moved into the caretaker's cottage to help out around the place. I believe in taking care of the people and things you have, not going out and buying new ones."

Maybe it would be better if she stopped asking him questions.

The rest of their trip was spent in silence.

Wade turned onto a short dirt road outside of town that led to a charming blue and white two-story farmhouse. Clay pots of colored flowers dotted the large wraparound porch.

A sign hung off the corner of the porch reading BAKER'S BED 'N' BREAKFAST.

Wade carried the dog and held the door for her as she entered the quaint house.

She found the country decor of overstuffed couches, quilted throw pillows, and antiques enchanting and itched to explore the dozens of books that filled the shelves lining the far wall.

The air smelled of vanilla and baking bread, and the tiny woman that bustled out of the kitchen had a smudge of flour on her cheek.

"My lands, child," the woman said, drawing her hand up to cover her mouth. "The judge called and told me he was sending over Bud and Dotty's granddaughter, but sakes-a-mercy, you're the spitting image of your mother."

A warmth filled her at the woman's words. Her dad rarely spoke of her mother. "Thank you. I miss her." Her words were soft, and she didn't quite know why she'd said that last part.

Something about this woman reminded her of her own grandmother.

"I bet you do. Your grandmother and I were friends for most of our lives, and I watched your mother grow up. She had a wonderful spirit, and I loved her as if she were my own." The woman crossed the room and engulfed Reese in a heartfelt hug. "You poor thing. It sounds like you've had quite a time of it today."

She almost came undone at the sincerity of the woman's words, and she wanted to stay wrapped in her cozy embrace.

It had been so long since she'd felt any kind of motherly affection, and she swallowed at the lump forming in her throat. "Thank you," she whispered, sinking into the hug and drawing strength from it.

The older woman patted her back then straightened

and narrowed her eyes as if taking stock of her appearance. "Think nothing of it. We'll get you fixed up here. You call me Miss Abigail." She lifted the bandage and peered at the cut on her head. "Looks like you conked your noggin a good one, but I've got some ointment and fresh bandages that I can send up to your room."

Miss Abigail was a tiny petite thing, but she ruled the room as if she were a General Staff Sergeant. Reese was pretty sure that Wade was going to be returning those panty hose, there was no way this lady was queen-size or tall.

He took the sleeve from his front pocket and dropped it on the table. "Reese grabbed you your hose for tonight."

"Oh thank you, sugar." Miss Abigail looked up at her with a mischievous grin. "I always like to buy them big otherwise they're so tight you need a forklift and some—"

"Don't say it," Wade interrupted.

Miss Abigail laughed. "Well, you know what I mean." She took the injured pug from Wade's arms then instructed him to take Reese's things up to the suite on the second floor.

She turned back to Reese. "I'll get your little poochie here some water. You follow my grandson up, and get out of those filthy clothes. I'll bring you some fresh towels and a couple of aspirin. Have you eaten? Never mind, I'll bring you a sandwich."

Wade bent to kiss the woman's wrinkled cheek with a murmured "Yes ma'am," before leading the way up the stairs and depositing her into a charming room that smelled of cinnamon and apples. A blue and white quilt covered the bed, and an overstuffed chair sat in front of the window.

"I adore your grandmother already," Reese told him.

"Yeah, me too. She's pretty great." He grinned then caught himself and returned to his former scowl. "I'll leave you to it," he said, before pulling the door shut behind him.

Reese looked around. The room was big, obviously

remodeled to combine two rooms into one large suite. A deep claw-foot bathtub sat in one corner of the room, and all she wanted to do was fill the tub with hot water and sink into its depths.

Five minutes later, she sighed as she sank into the sudsy bubbles in the bathtub, the warm water a balm to her aching and bruised body.

She knew she should probably be calling her dad and her clients and figuring out how she was going to take two weeks out of her life to fill her sentence. But she didn't want to think about that. Her clients would be fine, and since she hardly ever used it, she had plenty of vacation time saved up. She'd call in tomorrow and get someone to cover her appointments.

Her dad was going to be annoyed—he hated anything that messed up his perfect routine. Admittedly, she liked her own routine as well, and she really had no idea how she'd landed herself in this hot water.

She had no clue how she was going to rebuild the outhouse or get through the next few weeks of being in Cotton Creek. But she had been responsible for burning down the little outhouse, and she cringed, thinking about how much worse it could have been. She'd just have to suck it up and make amends.

Starting right after this bath.

For now, the soothing soak was just what she needed, and she gently pushed a swell of suds across the surface.

Her pink painted toenails peeked out of the water as she rested her feet on the edge of the tub and thought about the man whose jean-clad butt she'd just followed up the stairs.

She added his cute tush to the plus column as she tallied up her new guardian's qualities. He seemed kind-hearted—not to her, but to her dog and to his grandmother.

He was tall, and the muscles of his bare chest proved that he either worked hard or worked out.

Despite the scowl that he so frequently wore, he was a pretty decent-looking guy. She liked his messy blond hair and the scruff of beard on his chin. His eyes were blue, and she liked the way they sparkled with mischief when he teased his grandmother. He was cute.

Who am I kidding? He's hot.

Her pulse raced a little as she thought of him seeing her half naked as she'd stripped off her hose in the jail cell. His hands had been gentle as he'd tended her forehead, and she couldn't help but notice the way the muscles in his arms flexed and bulged when he'd been working to put out the fire.

Maybe she'd been looking at this all wrong.

Instead of seeing the next two weeks as a punishment, she needed to view her time spent in the tiny mountain town working with the hunky park ranger as an opportunity. A chance to try out her newfound freedom.

She didn't really know anyone here so there was no one to judge her or to tell her she failed. What better place to try out controlling her own life than with her love life? And it would stick it to Brock, too. Why not see what it felt like to be the one to start something new—and with someone she'd never met, who had no reason to believe that she would automatically bend to his will?

The more she thought about it, the more she liked the idea. She had two weeks to be someone new. A different Reese Hudson. Not the boss's daughter. Not Brock's arm candy. But who she wanted to be. To do what she wanted.

To act exactly how she felt at the time. To act out even. Yeah, maybe she needed to act out a little. Do something wild and totally out of character.

Thoughts of Wade's bare muscular chest filled her mind. Hmmm. Maybe a little acting out was *exactly* what she needed. And maybe Wade Baker was just the guy to act out with. She had two weeks of her *punishment*. Why not enjoy herself at the same time? Experience a little nature with an easy-on-the-eyes park ranger?

She considered her earlier list of requirements for the next man she got involved with. She already knew from the ride over here that Wade wasn't vain about what vehicle he drove, and he wasn't concerned about dog hair on his pants.

Yes, Ranger Baker would do quite nicely. He wore jeans, respected women, and was nice to her dog. Not to mention he had tight buns and abs of steel.

And she knew her dad would hate him. Which made her like him even more.

Now, she just had to convince the ranger.

A soft knock sounded on the door.

"Come in," she called, expecting Miss Abigail to bring in the promised towels.

The door opened, and Ranger Wade himself walked in, carrying a stack of towels and a sandwich on a plate.

His eyes widened as she shrieked and splashed water over the tub trying to cover herself. "Turn around! What are you doing?"

Wade abruptly turned his back to her, setting the sandwich and towels on the bench seat inside the door. "You said to come in. How was I supposed to know you were naked?"

She grinned at the strangled way he said *naked*. "Look, just keep your back turned and pass me one of those towels." She watched him take one of the thick towels and hold it out behind him. "I have a question for you, Wade. Do you own a suit?"

He walked backward toward her, the towel hanging from his outstretched hand. "You mean like to wear to funerals?"

Yes. Wade Baker would do just fine.

Now to convince him. First step to taking control. Here goes nothing.

And everything.

She stood up in the bathtub and reached for the towel.

But instead of seducing him with her slick suds-covered body, the quick motion suddenly had the sides of her vision closing in, and the last thing she saw was the floor rising up to greet her before everything went black.

. . .

"Holy hell!" Wade heard the splash of water as Reese stood up, then, from the corner of his eye, he saw her start to go down.

Quick reflexes had him reaching for her, and he caught her before she fell over the side of the tub.

But now his arms were full of a slick, naked, unconscious woman, and he froze, not knowing how to proceed.

How could he lift her out of the tub and not touch anything inappropriate? How could he preserve her dignity and not look when everything in him was dying for one glance?

He swallowed and took one quick peek at her pale skin and luscious curves as he tried to hold her up and reach for the towel he'd dropped.

Aw hell. This was stupid.

She was unconscious, and he needed to get her out of the bathtub before she fell back in and drowned. He scooped her body up and carried her to the bed, laying her gently down on top of the quilt. Grabbing the towel, he covered her then lifted her wrist to check her pulse rate.

Trained in first aid, he was sure the bump on the head combined with no food and standing too quickly had caused her to pass out. Her pulse beat steady.

She stirred, mumbling something about matching socks. Blinking her eyes, she looked around and struggled to sit up.

"Whoa there, missy. Lie still a minute. You just tried to get out of the tub, and you passed out."

She blinked again. Glancing down at her bare legs, she

gasped and clutched the towel to her. A pink tinge rose on her pale cheeks. "How did I…? Did you…?"

He nodded and tried to hold back the sheepish grin that threatened to spread across his face. "But I tried not to look. Mostly."

Mostly?" She arched an eyebrow at him, and he could swear her eyes had just the naughtiest gleam in them for a second.

Well, what do ya know about that?

She pressed up on her elbows, and drops of water from her hair slid down her skin. The bedding was soaked and he'd have to find her a new quilt for tonight.

He perched on the edge of the bed, moisture seeping through his jeans where her wet bare leg rested against his hip. Maybe the wet fabric would help cool his heating libido. It hadn't worked yet because he was still tempted to run his hand along her thigh. Test out if he really saw that gleam or if he'd imagined it.

He was certainly imagining things now. Like how soft her skin was, and what would happen if he reached under that towel. Would she let him, or would he earn a slap in the face?

He had seen her naked now. Better not push his luck. Besides, he'd already decided that he didn't want to get involved with another money-grubbing blonde.

He cleared his throat and stood up. "I better let you get some rest. Gram sent up a sandwich, and there are drinks in the mini-fridge. Help yourself. I'll bring you up some dry bedding, too. We should probably get an early start tomorrow. Should I pick you up at eight?"

"Make it ten, and I'll meet you up there. I'll need to take care of a couple of things in the morning."

Of course. He should have guessed. Already putting off the hard work. And messing up the schedule of his day. He had a feeling this wouldn't be the last time he made a change to please her.

Chapter Four

Wade couldn't believe his eyes.

He pulled into the parking lot of the falls at ten the next morning to find Reese sitting on a huge stack of fresh lumber, studying a thick sheaf of papers in her hand.

"What the heck is all this?" Slamming the door of the pickup, he side-stepped around two large bins, *Hank's Hardware* embossed on their sides.

Rounding the lumber, he was even more astonished to see a brand new stainless steel toilet perched on the ground next to the burned-out wreckage of the outhouse.

Reese grinned like the Cheshire cat. "Aren't you surprised? I got all the supplies needed to build a top-notch outhouse." She waved the stack of papers in her hand, obvious pride in her voice. "I googled how to build an outdoor toilet, and I found a list of supplies and the instructions I need to follow."

"Instructions? On how to build a toilet? Who uses instructions for that? You frame the room, replace the fixture and restock it with TP."

Her face fell, and her tone changed from pride to

defensiveness. "Well, some of us have never built an outhouse before."

He looked down at the bins full of new tools, nails, and hardware. "Do you even know what half this stuff is for?"

"No. But I stopped in at Hank's Hardware this morning and told him what I needed, and he was happy to load all this up for me, and even had one of his guys drive up here this morning to deliver it."

"I'll bet he did."

"What? Don't you like Hank? I thought he was great. Even put in some things I hadn't thought of, like an electric nail gun."

"Electric nail gun?" He looked around the forested area. "Just where do you plan on plugging that in?"

"Oh. Huh. I hadn't thought of that."

"I guess not." He could imagine when Hank saw Reese's platinum credit card that he threw in *several* extras. He was torn between feeling sorry for Reese and being glad that at least she'd helped the local economy of Cotton Creek and didn't get all this stuff delivered from one of the chain hardware stores in the city.

He walked around the pile of lumber. "What is this wood you've got?"

"It's composite decking lumber. Hank said it cost a little more, but it would hold up a lot longer and not need as much maintenance."

Hmmm. It irked him that she could so easily go out and purchase the best that money could buy, but it was good for the park to have the better material.

He looked toward the piles of used lumber filling the back end of his pickup. Too bad he'd spent the last hour scrounging lumber from the park's service shed.

He motioned for her to follow him as he headed for his truck. "I have a couple of things for you." He reached into the cab of his truck and handed her a worn leather tool belt. "Thought you could use this."

She grinned and raised her arms for him to fit it around her waist. "Nice. My first tool belt. I love it."

Oh man. He could just hand her the belt. It wasn't that hard to figure out. But then he would miss a chance to get his hands on her. She wore khaki shorts and a snug-fitting V-neck T-shirt that had *Baker's Bed 'n' Breakfast* scrolled across her ample chest.

She scooted closer to him, her arms still raised. He wrapped the belt around her waist, his long fingers moving treacherously close to her danger zone.

He liked the way she caught her breath, and her eyes went soft and sexy. Resting his hands on her hips, he regarded her for a moment.

She looked up at him, and he couldn't quite read what was in her green eyes. It felt almost like an invitation. Her lips parted and for an instant, he considered leaning down and kissing her. Taking that perfect little mouth with his. It'd be so easy.

He imagined pressing her against the truck, lifting her to draw those bare legs around his waist and laying claim to her lush curves. His hands itched to touch her, to run his thumb along her chin and draw her mouth to his. The scent of her shampoo enveloped him as he dipped his head slightly, eyeing her with a cross between a question and a dare.

Bark! Bark!

The moment was broken by the yap of the dog. Bagel was clawing at the half-open window, desperate to get out of the car and greet Wade.

"Bagel, stop barking," Reese called to the dog. She shrugged. "Sorry, I hate to keep him cooped up in the car, but I didn't want to leave him at the bed and breakfast."

"I might have something to help with that." Dropping his

hands, he reached into the bed of the pickup and lifted out a small wagon lined with a cream-colored sheepskin blanket. A small water dish was wired to the corner of the wagon. "I made this for the little guy so he could sit outside with us and not be contained to a crate. Plus he wouldn't get hot in the car that way."

Reese's hands covered her mouth as she gaped at the little wagon. "I can't believe you did this. This is so nice." A spark lit her eyes. "Let's try it out."

Racing to the car, she gingerly lifted Bagel from the front seat and set his chubby body down into the wagon, tucking his injured leg under him. "It's perfect."

She beamed at Wade, her bright smile making him feel like a hero. All he'd done was make a little dog cart.

Yet he practically tingled with pride as she threw her arms around his neck and planted a quick kiss on his cheek.

With her glowing at him like he'd just hung the moon and the way she was pressed against him, other things were starting to tingle, too.

What was this woman doing to him? All he could think about was laying her down in the tall grass and showing her what other things he could do with his hands. He needed to get this under control, and quick.

Clearing his throat, he unclasped her hands from his neck. "Well, you better get started. I don't have time to stand around here all day."

He pointed to the burned-out remains of the outhouse as she wheeled the dog over in the cart. "You're gonna need to start by tearing down the rest of that burned-up frame. Get everything cleared away until all you're left with is the concrete slab. Then you can start to rebuild on the slab."

"Got it." She nodded and went to work.

"You can pile it all up over here, and I'll have maintenance pick it up later." He headed for his truck. "I'll come back to check on you around lunchtime."

"Lunchtime?" Her face wore a bewildered expression, and she looked around as if searching for a fast food restaurant. "I didn't even think about lunch. Hey, wait. You're not staying? You're not going to help?"

"Nope. I'm just the supervisor." He chuckled and pulled a shovel and broom from the back of his truck. He laid them on the ground for Reese to use. "But Gram packed me a lunch big enough for four people so I'll be back around noon with some food. You're burning daylight, girl. You better get to it."

. . .

What nerve. Reese watched Wade's truck drive off leaving her in a cloud of dust and frustration.

Not only was he immune to her suggestive advances, he didn't even want to stick around to keep her company. She'd practically thrown herself at him, landing in his arms two different times, and he'd done nothing.

She'd been sure she'd seen a glimmer of arousal in his eye, but he hadn't taken the bait. Maybe he had a girlfriend or liked to take things slow. She'd planned on getting to know him as they'd worked together this morning. To figure out what made him tick. And what it would take to get under his skin—and under the sheets of his bed.

Ranger Wade had invaded her dreams last night, filling her head with erotic fantasies of him climbing in the tub with her and soaping up her dirty parts. She'd awoken to a mess of tangled sheets and a frustrated desire to get into the head and arms of the hot park ranger.

He hadn't exactly rebuffed her subtle advances, he just hadn't taken advantage of them. Or her. Maybe she needed to up her game. But how could she do that if he wasn't even around?

She hadn't dreamed that he would really let her do this all by herself. She stared at the wreckage of the little building. How the heck was she supposed to tear the rest of that thing down?

Her phone buzzed in her pocket, showing her dad's number. She'd called the office this morning and got her calendar covered, then left him a message explaining that she needed to take a few weeks off to clear her head. No reason to get him involved in this.

She'd made this mess, and she could clean it up. And what a mess it was. Letting loose a sigh, she dug through the box of tools, grabbed a hammer, and set to work.

Two hours later, the sound of a truck engine signaled Wade's return, and she stopped to survey what she'd completed. A large pile of scorched wood lay next to the parking lot, and she'd just finished sweeping off the concrete slab.

She winced at the fiery blisters bubbling on her palms and knew she must look a sight covered in soot and dirt from the boards. Her ponytailed hair was damp with sweat, but she felt good, like she'd really accomplished something.

Wade set a battered red cooler on the ground and surveyed her work. He looked surprised at all she'd finished. "Dang, girl. You've really been working. I didn't think you'd have half of this done. Good job."

He handed her an icy bottle of water, and she cringed as it touched her blistered hands. Wade frowned and pulled her hand to him. "Geez, look at your hands. Why didn't you wear gloves?"

She shrugged, not wanting to pull her hand out of his hold. "Hank didn't sell me any."

"The guy sold you an electric nail gun, but didn't get you any gloves? What a knucklehead." He strode to his truck, returning a minute later with a soft pair of leather gloves. "I'm sorry I didn't think to leave these with you earlier. I've got a little first-aid kit in my truck. I'll get you fixed up after lunch. You hungry?"

Her stomach growled at the mention of food. "Starving. I hope Miss Abigail packed a side of beef in that cooler. Although I don't know what that would leave you to eat."

He laughed, and the sound of it carried into her soul. Something about that deep chuckle had her insides doing a little flip.

She liked the easy way she could make him laugh and that he cared about her blistered hands. She adored that he was pouring more water into the dish for her dog to drink.

This guy might just be one of the good ones that she was always hearing about. He certainly looked good. Forget food, she could have Ranger Wade for lunch. And dinner.

Her stomach growled again. Okay, maybe forgetting food was a bad idea, but at least she would have a nice view while she ate.

Wade patted the stack of lumber next to him and handed her a sandwich as she sat down. He set out bags of chips, pickles, and cold soft drinks. Her mouth watered at the thick slices of roast beef and cheddar on a homemade roll, and she dug into the lunch as if she hadn't seen food in days.

Her phone buzzed again, bouncing on the planks of lumber where she'd set it earlier.

Wade watched her ignore the call then checked out the display. "Six missed calls from the CEO. Seems like your boss really wants to get ahold of you."

She sighed. "I left him a message that I won't be in for the next two weeks, and I'm not quite ready to tell him why."

"And the CEO cares if you take vacation days?"

"He does if he's your father."

"Ah. You work for your dad." He said the statement with a hint of disdain as if he'd just caught her stealing money from a tip jar.

A flicker of shame heated her cheeks. "I know. Pretty pathetic, huh?"

"No, I didn't mean that." At least he had the decency to look embarrassed. "Not if you like your job, I guess. What do you do?"

"I'm a financial planner."

"And do you enjoy it?"

"Not even one little bit." She plucked a chip from the bag and popped it in her mouth. "In fact, I pretty much hate that stinking job. I would rather be here, hauling away rubble and earning blisters the size of Texas than be at that job."

He laughed. "Then why don't you quit if you hate it that much? Do something else."

"Do we need to go back to that little part about my dad owning the company?"

Suddenly the taste of the chip went flat on her tongue, and she took a sip of soda to wash it down. "If I quit, I'd be letting my father down."

"Not if it were to do something you loved. Plenty of kids grow up to leave the family business. Is there something else you'd rather be doing? Why don't you just tell him you want to do a different job?"

This time it was her turn to laugh. "Yeah, right. I tried that once. When I first started college, I wanted to get a degree in journalism. I tried to tell my dad that I wanted to be a writer. And he laughed it off, like it was a big joke. Told me writing was a hobby that I could certainly pursue in my free time, but he'd already changed my field of study and sent my application to the School of Business where I would get a real degree in a field that would actually earn some money."

"Your dad sounds like a real piece of work." Wade tossed Bagel the last scrap of his sandwich. "So are you still writing?"

Images of the stacks of notebooks she had crammed with stories and plot ideas filled her head. Notebooks hidden in a chest at the foot of her bed. "I used to. All the time. I've even written a couple of books."

"Impressive. The most I've ever written is a grocery list. I think that's cool. Did you try to get them published?"

Her cheeks warmed at the compliment and the encouraging words about her work. "No. I thought about it though. I really loved writing."

"Then why'd you stop?"

Why *had* she stopped?

Writing was her passion, something she truly loved. But with work and Brock, there never seemed to be enough time.

She'd mentioned her writing to Brock once and received the same contemptuous response she'd gotten from her father. It just wasn't worth the hassle. It was easier to put her notebooks away and concentrate on her job at the company. "I guess my time got filled with other things."

Wade studied her face, and it was as if he could see right through her.

She squirmed under his gaze. "What?"

He shrugged. "You just looked so sad when you told me you don't write anymore. It seems to me if you love something that much and it makes you happy, then who cares what other people think, you find a way to do it. Why are you letting other people get in the way of your dreams?"

He had a point. Wasn't that the whole reason she'd broken up with Brock, to take control of her life? To do what she wanted and not spend all of her time trying to please everyone else. "You're right. Writing does make me happy. And I have this great idea for a book that's been bouncing around in my head for years."

"Well, there you go. Just remember me when you're rich and famous."

Yeah, like she was about to forget the hunky guy who landed her in jail and saw her naked in the same day. Except she'd been unconscious when she'd been naked so she didn't even get to enjoy it.

She grinned. "Now that we've solved all of my problems, let's work on yours. What can I do to help you with your troubles, Mr. Ranger?"

His eyes darkened, and a scowl crossed his face. "My troubles started with someone telling me a story, and they're not something you'd be able to fix, or even understand." He packed the rest of the trash into the cooler. "We better get back to work."

He tossed the cooler back in the truck, leaving her to wonder what she'd said wrong. They'd been laughing and joking around and then suddenly his mood shifted, as if he'd flipped a switch. Something about her set him off. And not in a good way.

Which made her even more resolved to figure out what was going on. One minute he looked at her as if he wanted to kiss her senseless, the next his gaze held contempt. And she was determined to find out why.

• • •

He couldn't take it anymore. After forty minutes of watching her clumsily lay out boards, thumb through her pages of instructions, and fail miserably at hammering a nail, he couldn't stand by and watch for one more minute.

Not that he hadn't enjoyed the view of her bending and stretching as she moved boards around and tried to lay out the frame. The woman had amazing legs, and all the right things jiggled when she swung the hammer. The tool belt he'd given her rode low on her hips and swayed as she walked past him.

A few times he'd thought she'd almost been adding a little extra sway when she'd sauntered past, bending to pick up a tool from the box, and he wondered if she were purposely putting on a show for his benefit. But why?

What purpose would she serve by getting a poor country boy all riled up when he was sure she could have rich men in the city bending to her every beck and call?

What did it matter? She was only here for a few weeks, then she'd be gone. Might as well enjoy the performance while he could. And he had a front row seat.

The scent of Reese's perfume wafted to him on the warm summer air, and that was it. "All right. I'll help you."

Her head snapped up, and he thought he saw a shimmer of relief in her eyes. Then she shook her head. "It's okay. I think I've almost got it figured out."

"You don't even have the measurements figured out yet." He grabbed his toolbox from the truck and instructed her to stand at one end of the concrete slab. Handing her the end of a tape measure, he measured and recorded the figures they would need to build the frame.

Patting the seat next to him at the picnic table, he drew up a quick sketch of the frame and added the measurements in. "We need to start from the ground up and build the frame. I don't know what you were doing over there, but you haven't even measured one thing."

She glanced at the disheveled pile of lumber on the slab. "I was eye-balling it."

He laughed. "Well, you might need a new pair of glasses, 'cause your eyeballs are sorely out of whack."

"All right, Mr. Handy Man, then show me how it's done."

He narrowed his eyes at her, wondering if she really meant the double entendre. He could show her how a lot of things are done, and he was quite *handy*.

In fact, he'd like to get his hands on her right now.

Geez, get it under control, man. If he kept thinking like that, he'd be adding extra wood to the already extensive pile they had. "Why don't you grab one of those two-by-fours? We can set it on the end of the table here, and I'll get it cut."

Using a hand saw, he cut the boards to the correct lengths, and they laid them out in a square on the concrete slab.

A grin covered her face as she pushed the boards together. "Hey look, a perfect fit."

"My grandpa taught me to measure twice, cut once." He'd had to measure three times on that board because Reese had leaned toward him to hold it in place, giving him a perfect view down the neck of her T-shirt. Her lush breasts spilled over the top of her white lace bra, and he completely forgot the numbers he'd just written down.

What was wrong with him? He was acting like a high school kid with his first crush. He was around women all the time. Why was he letting this one blonde get to him?

She was eager to learn, but her efforts were clumsy as she tried to carry out the tasks he taught her. He showed her how to hold a hammer and set the nail, her body resting snug back against his as he laid his hand on top of hers to demonstrate the swing of the tool.

She squirmed against him, and he almost came undone. "Why don't we take a break? Let's walk up to the waterfall. Stretch our legs a little."

They pulled the dog in the little cart up the path, and she pointed at the wildflowers growing along the trail. "I love these purple flowers, and those pink ones are gorgeous."

"The purple ones are tansy asters, and the others are called Indian paintbrush."

She looked up at him with a rapt expression. "Impressive. Do you know the names of all of them?"

He shrugged, acting like it was no big deal, but a small burst of pride swelled in his chest. Tawnya had always been embarrassed by his profession. "I better know what they are. I *am* a park ranger, you know. Part of my job is leading guided hikes and environmental education so I teach people about wildflowers and birds and survival skills."

Her face lit with excitement. "Oh, would you teach me some of them, please?"

They hiked up the path, her asking the names of every flower and him pointing out interesting nature facts and teaching her the names of the different plants.

Finally making it to the overlook, they stood at the railing in front of the soaring waterfall. Droplets of spray hit their faces, and Reese tipped her head back and closed her eyes. "I love this place."

"Me, too." He tore his eyes from the pale skin of her neck and focused on the rushing water. He leaned on the railing overlooking the falls. "So what were you so intent on destroying yesterday that you almost burned my park down?"

A faint blush crept up her neck. "Some stupid mementos from my ex-boyfriend."

"When did you break up?"

She consulted her watch. "About twenty-four hours ago."

"Ah. You seemed more angry than broken-hearted. Did he choose someone else?"

"Yeah, himself." She let out a sigh. "Brock cared more about himself than he did me. His needs always came first, and then he told me what I needed. It took me a long time to see that I have my own wants. My own needs. And he wasn't one of them. Neither he nor my father are very happy about my decision."

Wade's gut twisted as she spoke the words *wants* and *needs*. He'd known her such a short time, but he knew he wanted her already.

But needing her was a different story. He definitely did *not* need the complication of a woman on the rebound. A woman who lived a lifestyle that he couldn't even comprehend.

A spray of water shot from the falls, and Reese laughed and stepped back into him. His arms came up to steady her and then she was twisting, tipping her head up, her emerald-colored eyes shining with an invitation to take her.

And it was too much.

He pulled her to him, crushing her lips and filling his hands with her sweet, lush body.

She pressed against him, wrapping her arms around his neck and matching his desire with hers. She tasted like mint and smelled like summer.

And she felt so damn good.

Desire engulfed him, and he yearned to lay her in the grass and get her beneath him. To explore and touch her exquisite body. He ran his hands down her back, pulling her closer as he feasted on her mouth, giving way to the brazen thoughts that had consumed him all day.

He slid one hand up the back of her shirt. She moaned against his mouth, arching her back and pressing her breasts up. Her skin was soft, and he wanted to rip her shirt from her body and feel her bare flesh against his.

The scuffs of hiking boots in the dirt interrupted his thoughts, and he broke away from Reese as a couple of middle-aged women rounded the corner to the overlook.

Breathing hard, he nodded at the hikers, then turned toward the falls to hide his obvious arousal.

The women passed, and one gave him a knowing smile. She leaned into her companion as they walked by. "That's the kind of ranger I'd like to teach me about some birds and some bees."

Wade eyed Reese.

Her cheeks were flushed, and she wore an embarrassed grin. What had come over him? If those hikers hadn't walked up, he might have taken her in the grass.

He held up his hands. "I shouldn't have done that. I was out of line. I'm sorry."

"I'm not." She offered him a naughty grin. "That was

much more fun than holding the tape measure. Although I did notice that your measurement changed while you kissed me."

He laughed before he could stop himself. *Beautiful and funny*.

And if he were honest with himself, he wasn't really sorry, either. Sorry that he had to stop, maybe. And sorry that he'd started something that he wasn't going to be able to finish. Because this was a bad idea all around. "We'd better get back. I think we've done enough for today. I'll help you pack up, and we can start again tomorrow."

. . .

Reese could not figure this man out. He seemed attracted to her.

And what a kiss!

Her pulse quickened just thinking about it. Ranger Wade could have dragged her into the grass and shown her some wildlife, and she wouldn't have stopped him.

So what was going on with him? What made him go from cold to hot and back again?

He'd helped her load the building supplies into the back of his truck then told her he would meet her back there at nine in the morning before driving away. He was a no-show at dinner so she shared a quiet meal with Miss Abigail.

She thought she'd seen the end of Wade for the night but swore she could smell his aftershave when she walked into her suite after dinner.

The room was empty, but on her bed lay a leather-bound notebook and a pink pair of work gloves. A note was scrawled on a torn sheet of paper, and her breath caught in her chest as she read the words. "Once upon a time…what are you waiting for?"

What *was* she waiting for?

Chapter Five

The next morning, Reese was prepared. She'd thought she could impress Wade with her hardware store purchase yesterday, but that hadn't done it.

Today she was trying a new tact. Donuts. And coffee.

Seriously, who didn't like donuts and coffee?

She was convinced this would start them off on the right foot today. And she wanted to thank him for his gift.

She'd stayed up half the night scribbling out the first few chapters of the book that had been rattling around in her brain for the past year.

Who knew if it was any good? Who cared? It felt so good to be writing again. Like meeting up with an old friend. The kind of friend that you can go years without seeing and within minutes you're chatting and giggling like no time had passed at all.

Wade's truck pulled into the parking lot, and her heartbeat quickened in anticipation of seeing him. Even her palms were sweating.

Geez, why was she suddenly so nervous?

Oh yeah. Because the last time she'd seen him, he'd kissed her senseless. Kissed her with a fervor that had her ready to rip his clothes off and jump him in the woods. Just seeing his dirty blond hair through the windshield had her tingling with eagerness to be near him again.

He slammed the door to the pickup and ambled toward her, a slow grin forming on his face. And a box of donuts in his hands. He tipped the box at her. "I guess great minds think alike."

So much for plying him with baked goods.

But the funny things his grin was doing to her belly made the duplicate donut debacle totally worth it. "I thought I'd appeal to your sweet tooth. I brought powdered sugar, jelly-filled, and chocolate-covered. What'd you bring?"

He laughed, and she thrilled at the sound of his soft chuckle. At least he was smiling and in a happy mood today. So far, so good. "I brought glazed and maple-iced."

She patted the picnic table beside her. "Sounds like we've got the makings of a feast."

What she really wanted to feast on was him. To lick and taste and devour.

But she would settle for a glazed donut. For now.

She waved the pink work gloves at him. "I wanted to thank you for the gloves and the journal. That was really thoughtful."

He straddled the seat bench of the picnic table and picked up a donut. "Did you write anything in it last night?"

"Oh, yes." Her words came out in a rush as she told him about the story she had started and how excited she was to be writing again. She worked her way through a chocolate-covered donut and the rest of her coffee as she told him the basic plot lines and described her characters.

She stopped and took a breath. "Sorry, that was rude. I've been talking non-stop for the last ten minutes."

He grinned. "It's okay. I like it. I think it's great you're so excited about it."

"I am. My hands can't keep up with how fast my brain is thinking of ideas. And it feels different this time. Like this is a really good story."

"Good for you. Must be the mountain air." He reached up and brushed the side of her lip with his thumb. His touch sent a shock wave of thrills through her spine. "You've got a little chocolate there."

"Thanks." She watched as he licked the chocolate from the side of his thumb and felt her insides go as gooey as the sweet frosting he'd just swept from her lip.

Holy chocolate-covered hotness. She wanted this man.

He slapped the table, making her jump. "Well, we better get to work."

Yep. Work. That's just what she'd been thinking.

At least they'd made it through a full half hour without Wade's scowl returning. Now she knew donuts and writing were safe subjects.

They worked through the morning, keeping conversation light and easy. Wade explained the next step of what they were building, and she tried her best to keep up and follow his instructions.

So far, she'd hit her thumb with a hammer twice and accidentally stapled the hem of her shorts to a board. But they were making progress and the frame of the building was going up.

Stopping for lunch, Wade again brought out a spread of sandwiches Miss Abigail had prepared. His hand brushed hers as he passed her a sandwich and it sent a little tingle shooting through to her happy place.

In fact, every time he'd bumped her this morning or come in contact with her body, she'd felt a similar tingle.

She'd been waiting for him to bring up the kiss from the

day before, but so far, he'd acted like nothing had happened.

And maybe nothing had. For him. Maybe he kissed women like that all the time.

Only one way to find out.

"So, Wade, what's your story? Why hasn't a handsome bachelor like you been snapped up and married yet?"

He cocked his head at her, as if considering her question. "So, you're saying you think I'm handsome?"

She kicked out a foot at him. "Quit evading the question. Why haven't you married yet? Or are you divorced?"

"Nope. Not divorced. Just never quite made it down the aisle. Came really close once, even had a toothbrush and my own drawer at her place. But it didn't work out."

"Why not?"

"I couldn't give her the lifestyle she wanted." He waved a hand at the trees around them. "She was not impressed with the salary prospects of a lowly park ranger."

This woman sounded crazy. If she had Wade's toothbrush in her bathroom and his body in her bed, who cared what was in his bank account. "What difference does it make how much money you make?"

He raised an eyebrow at her. "Asks the woman driving a new Lexus?"

Touché.

"My dad bought me that car. I was happy driving my old Subaru, but he insisted."

"Yeah, and you wouldn't want to turn down the gift of a new car."

"It's not like that. You know my mom died when I was young. So my dad is just very overprotective. He kind of freaks out sometimes about something happening to me. It means something to him to have me driving a really safe car so it was easier to just take the car than hurt his feelings or cause him to worry about me."

"Have you talked to him yet? Told him about the sentence?"

"I left him another message." She'd purposely called when she knew he was scheduled to be in morning meetings. "I told him I was okay and just needed some time to think. You know, after the breakup and all."

"What's the big deal? Why don't you want to talk to him? You're a big girl. You can do whatever you want, right?"

Right? That's how it should be. And that's how it would be. Breaking up with Brock was the first step, and breaking free of her father the next.

She sighed. "It's not that easy. Besides, he adores Brock, my ex. He hired him last year, and Brock's one of the top financial advisors in the company."

"So, what's wrong with the guy? Your dad likes him, he makes a lot of money, seems like a good match. So the guy's a little stuck on himself, you sure you can't work it out?"

A *little* stuck on himself? That was an understatement.

"Look, I don't care how much money he makes. The guy tried to control my every move. What I ate, how I dressed. Everything in our lives had to be his way. And I did it, most of the time. It didn't matter to me if I wore red dresses instead of blue, and I'm not that picky of an eater, so I didn't care that he always chose the restaurant. But a few days ago, he crossed the line, and I'd had enough."

An angry glower crossed Wade's face. "Did he hurt you?"

"No." She liked the way he suddenly got protective of her.

"Are you scared of this guy?"

"No, of course not." Although she had flinched a time or two, not used to the angry words that Brock sometimes used to express himself, and not quite sure what he'd do if she defied his wishes. "He tried to give my dog away."

"What?" He looked down at the chubby little dog sleeping in the wagon he'd made. "This little guy?"

"Yep, that's the one." The anger she'd felt flowed through her again as she remembered walking into Brock's office and not quite believing what she was seeing. "He wanted me to move into his place, but he didn't like Bagel. He hated getting dog hair on his clothes, and heaven forbid if he got a drop of drool on him. He'd gone to my apartment and picked up Bagel after arranging for another employee to take him. He was shocked that I was upset because he'd arranged such a nice woman to take the dog off our hands. He was literally handing my dog over to a stranger when I walked into his office."

She took solace in the shocked look on Wade's face. "That's why I had Bagel with me the other day. I broke up with Brock right then, right in front of Margaret from accounting. Who, by the way, is a very nice woman and was quite disappointed to not get my dog. I brought Bagel back to my office and started throwing everything that reminded me of Brock into a box, then I just had to get out of there. I couldn't breathe. I put the dog in the car and drove up here. It's my favorite spot. The one place that always makes me happy."

The sound of a car pulling into the parking lot drew her attention. No way.

She couldn't believe her eyes. It couldn't be.

Brock's black Cadillac Escalade drove up and parked in the spot in front of their picnic table. It was as if saying his name had somehow conjured him.

Bagel let out a low growl as the door of the SUV opened and Brock stepped out.

She rose to her feet and shook her head, shocked and speechless that he could be here.

He walked toward them, a grin on his gorgeous face. He wore a black suit with a turquoise shirt and striped turquoise tie, and looked as if he'd just stepped off the pages of *GQ* magazine.

Everything about this man was perfect, from his thick black hair, to his dazzling white teeth, to his perfectly chiseled chin. His skin glowed with a healthy tan from playing tennis at the club, and he walked with the confidence of a man who had money and power.

He was panty-dropping gorgeous and could have had any woman, two at a time if he'd wanted.

Reese knew women threw themselves at Brock all the time, and she often wondered what drew him to her. She felt so ordinary compared to the other women in their lives.

Was it the appeal of her father's company or her willingness to consistently comply with his wishes that attracted him to her?

He appeared to take in the scene and an ugly sneer crossed his face. "Well, what have we here? Looks like a nice little picnic out in the woods." He regarded Wade with a condescending glance. "You decide to go slumming with the locals, Reese?"

She could feel Wade's back bristle as he rose from the table. He stood an inch or two taller but that didn't seem to affect Brock.

Reese stepped in between the two men. "What are you doing here? How did you find me?"

He looked down at her as if she were a disobedient child. "It wasn't that difficult. Your dad told me you'd come up here. Why? Were you trying not to be found?"

"As a matter of fact, yes. The point of getting away for a week or two is to actually get away."

Brock offered another disapproving look at Wade then took Reese by the arm. "You've been gone for three days. That's time enough for you to have had your little fun or whatever it is you needed to do up here. But now it's time to come home."

"I'll decide when it's time for me to come home, and I'm not ready to leave." She pulled at her arm, but Brock had a firm grasp.

Bagel let out another low growl, and Wade took a step forward. "I think you heard the lady."

Brock let loose a scornful laugh. "Who are you? And what could you possibly have to say about the matter?" He squinted at Wade's name tag on his uniform shirt. "Ranger Baker. Why don't you go ahead and take a hike, Mr. Ranger."

Wade moved a step closer. "Reese can make up her own mind if she wants to go with you, and I believe she said she wanted to stay. Now let her go." His voice held more than a hint of steel, and she glanced at him, mouth open.

Brock squeezed her arm tighter, not used to people questioning his authority. "Oh, listen to the tough guy. What are you going to do about it if I don't?"

Oh brother. She could choke on the testosterone flying through the air. "Brock, just let me go. You're being ridiculous."

Uh-oh. That was the wrong thing to say.

Anger flashed in Brock's eyes, and they narrowed as he looked down his nose at her. "*I'm* being ridiculous? What's ridiculous is the way you've lowered your standards. You want to stay up here with the common folks and spend your time with this redneck, be my guest." He let go of her arm and shoved her toward Wade.

Wade pushed her protectively behind him. "It's time for you to leave."

"Who's gonna make me?"

Oh for heaven's sake. Was this really turning into a schoolyard brawl?

Within seconds, the situation spiraled out of control.

She didn't see who touched who first, but suddenly the two men were shoving each other, and Bagel barked and tried to jump out of the cart.

This had to stop. She wanted to be in control of her own decisions, yet she couldn't even control this conversation.

She scanned the table for something to get their attention. Grabbing the pastry box, she threw the remaining donuts at them.

A maple-iced grazed Wade's forehead, leaving behind a smear of icing, and a shower of powdered sugar rained down on Brock and left a flurry of white dotting his suit.

Wade dropped his arms and stared openmouthed at her, while Brock could only stare at his suit in horror.

"Well, I guess we're all being ridiculous. I'm leaving." She lifted Bagel from the cart and stomped to her car. *What idiots.*

This was the first time she'd ever had two men fight over her, and she'd have thought it would feel great. But they weren't even fighting about her. It was just a pissing match to see who was more macho.

It didn't make her feel good, it just made her mad.

She peeled out of the parking lot, spraying gravel and leaving the two men covered in dirt and donut dust.

Chapter Six

Wade's stomach growled as he stomped into the bed and breakfast. Talk about a crappy day.

Reese had left him to clean up their work site, and when he'd finally made it back to his office, he'd found a stack of paperwork that he'd been neglecting the past few days to help her.

He'd thought he'd settled down, but just thinking about Brock had his chest tightening and his blood pressure skyrocketing. The nerve of that guy. What an ass. What could Reese have possibly seen in him?

Oh, yeah. A fat paycheck, a nice house, fancy cars, designer clothes. The list was endless. And it was everything he didn't have.

That guy's suit probably cost more than Wade made in a month. Why was he letting this wealthy douche-bag get to him?

He didn't even care about that stuff. He didn't want to wear a suit and he damn sure didn't need a membership to some fancy club. He was happy having a beer with the guys down at Creek's Tavern on Friday nights.

He worked hard, and he lived within his means. He could appreciate nice things, but he didn't *need* them to feel successful.

In fact, the first thing he did after Tawnya left was sell his truck. He used the cash to pay off one of the cards and drove around his grandpa's old truck to alleviate another payment.

Just thinking about Tawnya made his blood boil.

Why am I getting involved with another woman living an expensive lifestyle? I can't afford it, and I don't want that type of life.

Although Reese *had* specifically told him today she didn't care that much about money or living the expensive lifestyle. Maybe she wasn't entirely like Tawnya.

Or maybe he'd been distracted by her full lips and thoughts of kissing her, and she just hadn't shown her true colors yet.

His breath came in angry puffs as he stormed into the kitchen and found his grandmother at the table cozily handing a bowl of mashed potatoes to Reese.

That's just great. He couldn't even eat in peace.

Turning to leave, he was stopped by his grandmother's stern voice.

"Wade Baker, you get back here and sit down. I made fried chicken for supper, and I know it's your favorite."

His mouth watered at the smell of the crispy crust. Slumping into the seat across from Reese, he grudgingly accepted a plate from his grandmother.

"I heard you had a bit of a dust-up today with Reese's friend." Miss Abigail scooped a heaping pile of mashed potatoes on his plate then drenched them in gravy.

He took a bite of chicken, and his anger dissipated slightly. "You could say that. Reese's friend is a bit of an asshole."

Miss Abigail whacked his hand with the ladle and flecks

of gravy flew across the white tablecloth. "No swearing at the table."

"It's okay," Reese said. "Brock *is* an asshole." She pulled her hand back as Gram brandished the ladle toward her.

Wiping the gravy from his hand, Wade tipped his head to his grandmother. "Sorry, Gram. But the guy was a jerk. A lucky jerk. I really wanted to punch him in his smug face. I might have, too, if Reese hadn't thrown a box of donuts at us."

Miss Abigail's mouth dropped open, and she gaped at Reese. "You stopped a fight with a box of donuts?"

"Yeah, nothing like getting hit in the head with a maple-iced to take the fight out of a guy." He said the words and couldn't help the slow grin that crossed his face.

It *was* kind of funny.

The three of them stared at each other a moment, then Gram giggled, sending all three of them into a bout of laughter.

The tension eased, and Gram checked her watch. "Oh gosh, I need to be at a PTA meeting. I'll just leave you two to finish up without me." She winked at Wade then pushed back from the table, grabbed her purse, and scooted out the back door.

Wade reached for another chicken leg. "My grandmother never was one for being good at subtlety."

"Yeah, I saw the wink." Reese grinned at him. "Plus, I figured she was a little old for the PTA."

"Oh no, she's really going to PTA. She'll head over to her friend Winnie's house where they'll play Pinochle, Talk, and drink Amaretto Sours. It's their thing."

Reese laughed.

He liked her laugh. He liked the way her smile lit up her whole face. He liked her. And that was the problem.

He just simply liked being around her.

So why did this have to be such a problem? Why couldn't they just hang out together and have a good time? Maybe he was letting his bias against females and money cloud his judgment of Reese.

Had he really even given her a chance? It couldn't hurt to just spend some time getting to know her. Could it?

He leaned back in his chair, regarding her. "So, what do you like to do for fun, Ms. Hudson?"

She narrowed her eyes as if she wasn't sure if he was serious or giving her a hard time. "Not much. I'm fairly boring. Most nights I read, watch a movie, or take my dog for a walk. Or sometimes I get crazy and do all three in one night."

He grinned. "That does sound pretty crazy."

Although his idea of a crazy night with her was something completely different.

"How about you? What do you like to do for fun?"

It sounded as if she added just the teeniest bit of tease to that question, but he couldn't tell for sure. Maybe it was just his own thoughts going into overdrive. "I guess I like to tinker around my grandpa's garage, hike, get out and enjoy nature, and I spend a fair amount of time fishing. Have you ever been?"

"Fishing? No, but lately I've decided that I need to try more new things."

"Yeah? I was thinking about doing a little night fishing after supper. Want to come along?"

"Sure. I'd love to go fishing with you."

. . .

What the hell had she been thinking?

I'd love to go fishing with you?

She thought he was flirting with her. Like fishing was some kind of code for making out.

No, he'd really meant fishing. Like, for actual fish.

She swatted at a mosquito as she trudged through a

pasture of waist-high grass carrying a smelly box. At least the view was good.

In the dim light of the moon, she kept her eyes trained on Wade's cute butt as they crossed the meadow behind the bed and breakfast.

"It's right up here." Wade unhooked the latch of a gate and held it open for her.

She stepped through the gate and gasped as she took in the charming setting. Cottonwood trees surrounded a small lake that dazzled in the moonlight, the chirping of crickets the only sound in the still night. "It's beautiful."

"Yeah, it is." Wade took her hand and pulled her out on the short dock where a rowboat was tethered. He climbed into the boat, setting the poles down first, then reached to help her step in.

She loved the feel of his hand on her back as he guided her into the boat. He was so at ease as he unhooked the rope and sat down on the bench across from her.

She liked this Wade. This happy guy that liked to fish. She liked his easy smile and the way his hair fell over his forehead. And she *really* liked the way his muscled arms flexed and tightened as he rowed the boat into the middle of the lake.

In fact, a few of her parts were tightening inside as she watched him move back and forth in the seat with the rhythmic pull of the oars.

Suddenly fishing didn't seem so bad.

He stopped the boat in the middle of the lake then instructed her to carefully turn sideways on the bench seat. He eased onto the seat behind her, straddling the bench with his legs, and nestling her bottom against him, then handed her a fishing pole. With his arms around her from behind, he helped her thread a worm onto the hook and toss the line into the water.

In any other instance, a gooey bloody worm being strung

on a hook would probably have grossed her out completely. But she didn't even notice.

All she could focus on was the way his thighs tightened against hers as he moved and the way his breath felt against her neck as he concentrated on the hook.

She turned to look up at him, squirming a little against him. "Aren't you going to fish?"

She didn't mean for her voice to come out quite so breathy. It was just that she didn't seem to have any breath left. Seeing his eyes go soft and his slow sexy grin seemed to have taken it all away.

"I'm happy to watch you." He cleared his throat. "Watch you fish, I mean. This way I can help you if you catch one."

Turning in the seat, she pulled her leg across the bench so she was facing him. She knew her hip grazed against him with the movement and reveled in the quick intake of his breath.

Where had this brazen little minx come from?

Her goal had been to turn over a new leaf, to take control of her decisions, her actions, her life. She was ready. In the still of the night, on a glassy lake sprinkled with stars and moonlight.

She couldn't have imagined a more romantic setting. Except for the whole fishing pole with a dead bloody worm on the end, it was almost perfect.

This was what she deemed a *moment*. An instant where time stands still and everything feels exactly right. She was going for it.

She rested one hand on Wade's muscled chest and traced his jawline with her other. Saying nothing, she was sure he could hear the fierce pounding of her heart in the quiet night.

He stiffened but didn't pull back.

She couldn't tear her gaze from his and leaned closer, gently grazing her lips against his. Sliding her hand up his chest, she cupped his neck, drawing his mouth closer to hers.

Hesitating, she felt him hold back, as if trying to decide if this was a good idea or not, but only for a second, then his arm slid around her waist and pulled her tight against him.

His mouth crushed hers in a kiss filled with desire and hunger.

She kissed him back, matching his passion, lost in the heat of the moment.

The fishing pole clattered to the floor of the boat then both of his hands were on her, touching, squeezing, caressing her body.

Crazed with a desire to get closer to him, she lifted his T-shirt, and he leaned back and yanked it off.

Grasping the hem of her shirt, he pulled it over her head and tossed it in the bottom of the boat. He dipped his head, grazing the tops of her breasts with his lips as his fingers easily unclasped her bra and slid it off.

Holy mother. She'd never done anything so bold in her life.

She was half naked in the middle of a lake, and she couldn't care less.

The only thing she did care about was getting closer to this man. She arched her back and pressed tighter against him, clutching his muscled forearms as he took her pert nipple between his lips.

A soft moan escaped her lips, and she was lost.

Lost in his touch, in the caress of the warm summer night's air against her skin, lost in the moment of pure bliss. Of the pleasure of a man's lust as he desired her.

A whirring sound filled the air, and his hands froze on her back.

"Holy crap! You got a fish!" He scrambled on the floor of the boat for the fishing pole, grabbed it and reeled in the line. "Grab that net."

Seriously?

She was half naked and sitting between his legs, and he wanted her to help him catch a fish?

She looked up at him and had to grin at the huge smile on his face. He was really excited about that fish.

"Come on, baby. It's a big one. Hurry, get the net, before he gets away!" He stood up in the boat, coaxing the line as he braced his legs on either side of the bench.

She scrambled from the seat and grabbed the net. "Got it."

Turning, she held up the net just as Wade swung the fish out of the water and landed it right in her lap.

Letting out a shriek, the slimy fish wriggled against her bare skin, and she flailed her arms, scrambling back.

Her sudden weight shift tipped the boat, and before she could regain her balance—she and the fish fell backward into the water.

"Hang on," Wade called, reaching for her.

She splashed and sputtered, the cool water an instant shock to her system. Taking in a deep breath, she got her bearings and swam to the side of the boat. It was a warm night and despite the wound to her pride, she wasn't hurt.

In fact, the whole thing was kind of funny.

Especially the look of concern in Wade's eyes as he leaned over the side of the boat to drag her in. "Are you okay?"

Actually a late night swim wasn't a bad idea.

"I'm good. The water's fine. I think you should join me." She reached for Wade's hand and gave a tug, pulling him into the water with a splash.

Oh my gosh. What had she done? What a stupid idea.

She held her breath, nervous as she waited for Wade's reaction. Brock could barely handle a speck of lint on his jacket, he would have had a fit if his clothes got soaked.

Wade popped out of the water with a whoop and shook the water from his hair.

His hearty laugh rang out in the still night, and her whole body relaxed as he grinned at her.

Then her heartbeat ramped up as he swam toward her, his grin going slow and sexy.

Oh boy.

He swam up next to her, his bare chest just inches from hers. "That was a pretty big fish you just cost me. Got any ideas how you're going to make that up to me?" His eyes held the hint of a dare, and she swallowed, her mouth suddenly dry.

You are in control. You got this.

Her self-talk rang in her head as she looped an arm around Wade's neck, drawing her body closer to his.

The full moon shone high in the sky and sparkled off the water, making it bright enough to see him, yet still dark enough to lend an air of romance and seclusion.

His Adam's apple bobbed in his throat as he glanced down at her bare chest floating in the water. And she knew she had him.

Sometimes men were so easy. All it took were boobs.

Then any thoughts she had disappeared in a haze of desire as he leaned in and kissed her. Kissed her with a fiery passion that all the water in the lake couldn't put out.

Her legs wrapped around his bare waist, and he treaded water to keep them afloat as his mouth devoured hers.

She tipped her head back, and he laid a hot line of kisses down her throat, his mouth warm against her lake-cooled neck.

The night air was warm, and the lake softly rippled. Moonlight and stars danced across the ripples, and she gazed across the water.

She froze. "Snake."

Wade laughed. "I guess you could call it that, but I promise it won't bite."

Her paralysis broke as she shrieked and splashed toward

the boat. "Holy shit! No—a big snake. A real one. On the water." She grabbed the sides of the boat and tipped it toward her, but she wasn't strong enough to get herself in.

With a few big strokes, Wade was at the boat and pulled himself up and over the edge. He reached down for her and tugged her up.

She collapsed on the bench seat, shivering. Her shirt and bra floated in the water filling the bottom of the boat.

She pointed at the snake on the water and panic filled her voice. "It's swimming this way."

Wade picked up the oar and brandished it at the snake. "Don't worry. It's probably just a bull snake."

"Probably?"

The snake swam up to the oar, and Wade lifted it on the end of the paddle. Reese shrieked as he swung the oar and flung the snake across the water.

He sank onto the bench seat and wrapped an arm around Reese's bare shoulders. "It's gone now. You okay?"

She nodded, her teeth chattering, but managed to give him a smile. "You are now officially my hero."

He chuckled and puffed out his chest. "You may call me the Snake Slinger." He picked up the now snake-free oars and with swift, hard strokes, rowed them quickly to the dock. "We can head back to the B and B, or I have a little fishing shack out here. I can build us a fire and see if I can't find you a shirt."

She wasn't ready to go back to her room, not when the night had just been getting good. "A fire sounds good."

He fished her wet shirt and bra off the bottom of the boat and passed them to her with a sheepish grin. "I kind of like this topless fishing idea. I think it could really catch on."

She held the wet shirt across her chest and had to laugh. "That would bring a whole new meaning to the term *fly fishing*."

He laughed and helped her from the boat.

Her tennis shoes made a squishing sound as she walked across the deck. He pointed at a small lean-to a few yards down the lake. Stacks of wood lined one side of the shack, and a fire pit sat in front under the wooden awning.

Wade disappeared into the shack, emerging moments later with a blanket and some towels. He passed her a large beach towel, and she wrapped it around herself.

After spreading the blanket on the ground by the fire pit, he gestured for her to sit as he grabbed a handful of wood. "Have a seat. I'll have a fire going in a sec, and we'll get you all warmed up."

She sat on the edge of the blanket and watched him work. Seeing his muscles flex and bulge as he stacked the wood was starting to warm her up already. Within minutes, a fire popped and crackled. Wade dropped down beside her and wrapped an arm around her shoulders.

Wearing only his shorts and an old pair of tennis shoes, he was the epitome of sexy, and she leaned into his hard muscled chest.

She was so completely out of her element. She'd never gone camping, never been fishing. Yet right here, right now, everything felt completely right.

Like this is exactly where I'm supposed to be.

Wade looked down at her. "You okay? Warm enough?"

She looked at his lips, and a warm heat moved through her that had nothing to do with the fire.

She wanted him.

He was the opposite of Brock in every way. Wade was kind-hearted and thought of her needs before his own. He was relaxed sitting bare-chested in the dirt, and she'd wager he didn't own a single bottle of hair product. And he liked her dog.

Besides all that, he seemed to actually like her.

She may have just won him over. All it took was a cold

dunk in the lake in the middle of the night.

No wonder she'd had bad luck with men. She'd been going about it all wrong.

Now was the time to get it right. She may have been in his world, but she was on her terms. She could have control of this situation. She just had to take it. Make a move.

Reaching up, she ran her finger down his cheek and across his lips. She reveled in the way he sucked in his breath. She traced a line down his neck and along his muscled forearm.

Peeking up at him from under her lashes, she offered him a teasing grin. "So, how do you feel about topless camping?"

She leaned back and dropped the towel from her shoulders and gloried in the look of pure desire that flashed in his eyes.

"I'm a huge fan," Wade said, his voice low and gruff.

He slid an arm around her waist, drawing her into his lap. Cradling her against him, he leaned in and kissed her, gentle and slow. He ran his hand through her damp hair, then trailed his fingers lightly down her back.

Shifting his position, he twisted and laid her gently on the blanket beneath him.

Then he proceeded to start a slow, agonizingly sweet exploration of her body with his hands, his lips, and his tongue. Every touch sent waves of pleasure rocking through her body.

He was so different from Brock. Her ex was so handsome and used to taking what he wanted. At times, he acted like having sex with him was a reward he'd bestowed upon her.

As if getting to fondle his mediocre-sized package was a prize she'd won in a contest.

Wade treated her as if she were a gift presented to him that he got to lovingly unwrap. He savored her body as if she were his favorite food, and he didn't want to rush the meal. Every lick, every taste, each delicate nibble, he feasted on her with a ravenous but skillful appetite.

Her outstretched hands gripped the blanket as he teased her belly button with his tongue.

Unsnapping her shorts, he eased the damp fabric down her legs. He pulled her panties off as well, leaving her naked underneath him.

The cool breeze whispered against her heated flesh, reminding her that they were outside, in the middle of a field, and she was completely naked.

And she loved it.

Her inner minx had awakened inside of her, and she reveled in the act of doing something so brazen, so unlike her normal self.

Her usual routine of getting ready for sex with Brock involved getting undressed and folding her clothes neatly on the chair by her bed.

And now, she didn't even know where her bra was.

It could be floating on the lake for all she knew. The fish that got away could be fighting over it with the snake.

Speaking of snakes.

Wade had somehow lost his shorts, and he knelt in front of her, his body strong and muscled and well-endowed. Like *really* well-endowed.

She thought back to his earlier claim of being called the Snake Slinger and thought his title may be true in more ways than one. And hoped she was about to find out.

His skin was tanned, and his blond hair seemed to glow in the firelight. Every part of his body was taut and toned. But his powerful physique came from working hard and hiking through the mountains, not from a gym.

He was so damn good-looking.

She reached up and ran her hands across his chest, rubbing his tight little nipple with her thumb.

Smiling at his quick intake of breath, she thrilled at the soft moan of pleasure that escaped his lips.

He grinned down at her. "Is it weird that I like that?"

She shook her head and pressed up on her elbows. "If you like that, you'll love this." Circling his nipple with her tongue, she raked her teeth across the nub and was rewarded with another groan, and she felt his hand tighten on her hips as he drew her closer.

She leaned back and grinned up at him, enjoying the fact that she could pleasure him with such a simple thing.

Lying bare before him, she hoped the dim glow of the fire hid her trouble spots. Like her too-soft belly that suffered from her lack of commitment to sit-ups and her fondness for ice cream.

Knowing her ample chest was one of her best assets, she loved the way his eyes were daring and sexy as they took in her nakedness.

Wade grinned back then leaned down, his voice low and husky. "I do like that. Now let's see if you do."

Oh. My.

• • •

What was this woman doing to him? Something about Reese Hudson had fried his brain and turned him into a sex-starved teenager.

He could not get enough of her.

Wade wanted to explore every inch of her luscious body. Seeing her naked and welcoming on the blanket beneath him drove him mad.

Her hair was still a little damp and curled slightly in a halo around her head. And she had this look that was a mix of *I want you* and *come take me*.

He almost had a heart attack when she'd dropped the towel and offered her topless self to him. Like seriously, he thought his heart might have actually stopped beating.

Her body was glorious. And he wanted it. Wanted her.

Like nothing he had ever wanted before.

He swallowed at the emotion rising in his throat as he stared down at her. "You are beautiful, Reese." Her eyes went round with surprise, and he wondered if she hadn't heard that enough. "And you are making me crazy with how much I want you."

"Oh, I passed crazy about five minutes ago." She gave him a naughty grin. "I've moved on to senseless and am almost at completely irrational."

He grinned back. "That sounds like a challenge."

Leaning down, he laid a soft line of kisses along her neck. He loved to hear her soft sexy moans of desire and to feel her buck up against him.

Taking it so slow was killing him. But in a good way.

Giving her pleasure was a total turn-on for him. He wanted to draw out her pleasure. Make her ache with need for him.

Her legs were wrapped around his waist, tightening with each shiver he caused. Raised on his arms above her, he couldn't get enough of looking at her body. Her breasts were perfect, lush and full.

He tipped his head down and ran his tongue lightly around her pert pink nipple before drawing it into his mouth.

He heard her sharp intake of breath and felt her thighs tighten.

Every instinct in him wanted to take her, to devour and sate his ravenous appetite. But instead of taking, he slowed his breathing and indulged in the moment, the feelings of pure carnal lust that he had for this woman.

He licked and nibbled, thrilling at her cries of longing. Touching and tasting, he explored the lush landscape of her curves.

Time held no meaning as she arched and writhed beneath

him. Finally, he reached the edge, no turning back. "I want you, Reese."

"Yes," was all he heard, and he sat up and reached for his shorts. Tugging his soaked wallet from his pocket, he grinned as he pulled a foil-wrapped condom from its folds. "Not only am I a park ranger, I was also an Eagle Scout. And you know the Boy Scout motto is *Always Be Prepared*."

Although nothing had prepared him for this woman laughing beneath him, her eyes shining in want and desire.

He ripped open the packet and took care of business before leaning over her and nuzzling into her neck.

Her hair brushed against his already inflamed skin, and his control slipped another notch. Unable to take another second, he reached down and cupped her bare butt as he pressed into her soft, warm center.

Her hands clutched his back as she moaned his name.

With the fire sizzling and popping behind them, he fell into a slow rhythm, increasing with her demands for more. He buried his head in her neck, inhaling the sweet scent of her skin.

He kissed her, taking her mouth in an assault of passion and need.

The darkness enveloped them and all that mattered was this moment. This perfect moment with Reese beneath him, matching his pace, then building the intensity.

His breath came in quick gasps, and he slid his hands down her body to grip her perfectly rounded ass.

She tightened under him, crying out as her body abandoned itself to the pleasure, and he lost himself in the release of heat and desire.

• • •

Oh. My. Gosh.

Reese struggled to catch her breath as Wade collapsed onto the blanket next to her. He pulled her into the crook of his arm in an affectionate embrace as she snuggled into the side of his chest, her body still quivering with sweet convulsions.

Holy hot ranger!

That had been amazing.

She never knew it could be like that. Wade made her feel like a treasure he had discovered. As if every part of her body was a new reward, a new gem to be marveled at and cherished.

And Lord, when he found the crown jewel, he really knew how to relish that prize.

"You warm enough?" he asked as he tightened his arm around her.

She nodded against his firm chest. "Yeah, I'm plenty warm. And you are seriously hot. Who knew getting back to nature could be so much fun?"

He gave her a crooked grin. "Oh, I have lots of ideas for other outdoor activities that I could show you. And the topless part is optional."

She grinned back. She couldn't wait to see what other ideas he had and what else he had to show her.

Chapter Seven

Wade whistled as he walked into the kitchen and grabbed a coffee cup. Nothing could hamper his mood today.

Last night with Reese had been amazing, and he felt on top of the world. Not even the light drizzle of rain could dampen his spirits.

He leaned down and dropped a kiss on his grandmother's head. "Good morning, Gram."

"You're certainly chipper this morning." She gave him a knowing look. "Reese told me that you took her fishing last night. Did you reel her in?" Miss Abigail giggled.

He arched an eyebrow at his grandmother before reaching for the coffeepot.

"You both just seemed really happy this morning. Like maybe you gave our guest some special *room service* last night?"

His hand stopped midway through pouring a cup of coffee. "Gram, quit talking like that. You have such a dirty mind."

Although she wasn't that far off track.

He'd dropped Reese off at her room last night fully intending to kiss her good night and let her sleep.

But one kiss had turned into two and then into three and then into eight. She'd gripped handfuls of his shirt and pulled him into her room, tugging their clothes off as they'd fallen onto the bed.

And that's where they'd stayed until after midnight, when he'd kissed her forehead and left her asleep as he headed out to his cottage.

"Where is Reese? I just knocked on her door, and she didn't answer." He filled a plate with biscuits and ladled gravy from the pan on the stove. He was famished this morning.

"She said for me to tell you that since it was raining, she figured you weren't going to work this morning, so she was going into town to the coffee shop to write. She said she'll hook up with you at lunch, though."

His pulse quickened as he thought about *hooking up* with her. Thoughts of her naked in his bed filled his mind. Images of her blond hair spread across his pillow and her bare skin against his.

He cleared his throat and sat down at the table across from his grandmother. Her head was bent over an electronic device, her concentration focused on the screen. "Whatcha got there, Gram?"

"It's one of those fancy iPads."

"Where did you get an iPad?"

"Reese gave it to me. She taught me how to check my email and how to crush these candies. It's quite addictive."

Reese gave it to her? An iPad?

His perfect mood shattered as reality came crashing down, and the all-too-familiar scowl returned to his face. "That's a pretty expensive gift, Gram. Are you sure she gave it to you, not just let you borrow it?"

"I'm sure. She registered it in my name and helped me

download some apps she thought I'd like." Her eyes stayed focused on the device, her finger swiping the screen as she absently answered. "Don't worry. She can afford it."

Yeah. That was the problem. She could afford it, and he couldn't.

He would have loved to buy his grandmother expensive gifts. Except, oh yeah, all of his money was currently being spent on another woman's debt. Another woman that liked expensive clothes and fancy purses and high-priced electronics.

How could he have let himself get drawn in again to a woman who made him feel like a prince in the bedroom but a pauper everywhere else?

His head tried to stick up for Reese, telling him that she wasn't anything like Tawnya, but his heart refused to hear it.

The shattered parts of his vulnerable heart railed against ever believing in another woman, especially one that doled out expensive gifts as easily as candy.

This was more evidence that Reese was used to a certain lifestyle. A lifestyle that he would never be able to give her. Tawnya's words of his inadequate earnings came rushing back, and the biscuit he'd just eaten turned leaden in his stomach.

He pushed his plate away, his appetite gone. "I'm going out to the barn, Gram. Have fun with your iPad."

Sarcasm dripped from his voice, but his grandmother failed to notice, her concentration still on the candy game. He slammed the back door as he headed outside.

He filled his morning with mundane tasks that involved little concentration but a lot of banging and hammering. He'd just finished repairing an old gate when Reese's Lexus pulled into the driveway.

Seeing the pricey car only fueled his anger, and he had a full head of steam on by the time Reese got out of the car and headed toward him. Her face glowed with happiness, and her eyes shone with excitement as she bounded toward him.

For a minute she looked as if she were ready to throw herself into his arms, but stopped short as she took in his angry expression and guarded stance.

"Uh-oh," she said. "The scowl is back. What's wrong?"

How could she be so blasé? As if everything was fine. "What's wrong is that you bought my grandmother an iPad."

A look of confusion crossed her face. "Well, I *gave* your grandmother an iPad. But why does that make you mad? Are you afraid your gram is going to look at internet porn?"

Her lighthearted joke fell flat, doing nothing to ease the anger and infuriation filling his chest.

She reached out to touch his arm but he pulled back. "Seriously. Why are you so angry?"

Why was he so angry? He'd been wrestling with that question all morning. What was the big deal if Reese wanted to buy his grandmother a gift?

Why was he so tied up in knots?

Because it wasn't about the gift. It was about the money and the fact that he didn't make enough of it.

That *he* wasn't enough.

"Just tell me why? Why would you buy my grandma such an expensive gift? Were you trying to show off your wealth? Or trying to show me up?"

A hurt look filled her eyes. "Of course not. I'm not like that. I thought you knew enough about me by now to know I'm not that kind of person."

He dragged his hand through his hair and let out a sigh. "I do know that. Or thought I did. That's why I was so surprised this morning when I saw that you'd bought it."

"First of all, I didn't *buy* it for her. I gave it to her. And if you would have actually looked at it, you would have seen that it's the earlier version. I got an upgraded one through my job and didn't need the old one. Because of the relationship with my grandma, Miss Abigail has been letting me stay here for free. I wanted to do something nice for her, and I thought she would get a kick out of it."

His anger deflated.

She wasn't trying to flash around her wealth. She was doing something nice. She was nothing like Tawnya.

He took a step toward her, ready to pull her into his arms, needing to feel her against him. The sound of a truck coming down the driveway stopped him, and he looked up to see the mailman pull to a stop in front of them.

Don, the mail carrier, waved as he hopped from the vehicle. "Hey, Wade. Do you have a guest staying out here named Reese Hudson?"

Reese stepped forward. "That's me."

"You must have gone on quite a shopping spree there little lady." The mailman grabbed several boxes from his truck and filled her arms with the packages. With a wave, he climbed back into his truck and drove off.

Wade shook his head. It looked like she had gone on quite a shopping spree. And he had been so close to accepting her casual explanation.

Thank goodness Don showed up when he did, with the proof of what she was really like. It was just as he thought.

He couldn't take this. Looking at Reese standing there, her arms laden down with boxes, gave him a physical pain in his chest. As if someone had taken hold of his heart and was ripping it in two.

"Tell Gram I'll be back later." Crossing to his truck, he yanked open the door. He took one quick glance back. "Have fun with all of your stuff."

• • •

Reese didn't know what to expect the next morning when she

showed up to work on their project. She hadn't seen Wade since he'd driven off in a huff the day before. She'd watched for his truck but never saw it return so she spent the rest of the rainy afternoon in her room, working on her book.

Miss Abigail had bingo so she'd left a note and a plate of lasagna for Reese for supper.

She'd finally heard Wade's truck pull in around ten o'clock, but decided it was too late to approach him that night.

Besides, what if he'd been cooling his heels with a woman from town? A guy that good-looking had to have plenty of women who would be willing to nurse his wounds. Her heart ached at the thought of another woman caring for Wade. And that was a problem, too.

Her heart wasn't supposed to be involved at all.

She never expected to actually have feelings for the guy. To lie in bed at night and think about his smile and the way his hands felt on her skin. To relive the tingly feelings she got as he kissed that perfect little spot under her ear.

She liked the way he held doors for her and asked for her opinion. He didn't make decisions for her, didn't act like he automatically knew what was best for her. She liked that.

She liked him.

That's why her palms were sweating, and her heart raced as she pulled into the lot and saw his park service truck. She knew she liked him, and thought he liked her, too. But something about her set him off. She just couldn't figure out what it was.

She was about to find out.

Slamming the door of the car, she cautiously approached Wade. He was working on the frame of the building and the sound of his hammer pounding a nail rang out in the forest.

Reese sucked in her breath. He was so hot. How did she ever get the interest of a guy like that?

And how could she get it back?

"Hi." She wore jean shorts, a white tank top, and the new pair of hiking boots that had been in the boxes she'd received yesterday. Her long hair hung loose and curled around her shoulders.

Hey, a girl's gotta use what she has. She'd tucked a ponytail holder in her pocket in case she needed it later.

Wade gave her a quick glance, then continued to hammer, the scowl never leaving his face. "Where's Bagel? His leg isn't messed up, is it?"

This was why she liked him. His first question was about her dog and if he was okay. "He's fine. Miss Abigail asked if he could keep her company today. I'm sure she'll spoil him all day with cuddles and sneak him bits of food. Like that dog needs any more food."

Her lighthearted joke fell flat as he continued his task. "Why don't you grab some gloves and hold that board up over there. We missed a day of work yesterday, so we need to make up for it today."

Resigned, she pulled out her gloves and crossed to the board he'd gestured to.

They worked through the morning, their silence broken only with bits of instruction from Wade. Her concentration was off and so far she'd nailed a board upside down and given him the wrong measurements twice.

She kept waiting for him to tell her why he was so mad at her. Or at least give her a hint. She was so used to Brock explaining in exact detail what she did to upset him that she couldn't figure out how to deal with Wade. Should she try to confront him and risk him getting angrier or just keep waiting for him to throw her a crumb of explanation?

She didn't know the answer, but she knew the silent treatment was killing her.

Finally, she couldn't take his scowl anymore. Either he liked her or he didn't. Tired of tip-toeing around his anger, she needed to know what was going on.

What had she done to cause such a shift in his mood?

She dropped her gloves on top of the cooler. "Let's take a break. I'm going to walk up to the waterfall. Would you like to come with me?"

He sighed and ran a hand through his hair. "Yeah, sure. It wouldn't hurt to stretch my legs a bit."

They walked up the trail and stood at the railing, soaking up the peace that she knew the water brought to both of them.

She tried to touch his hand, but he pulled it away. "All right, enough already. Would you just tell me what's wrong?"

He stared out at the waterfall.

Glancing around, she wished for a place to sit and talk. "It would be so great if there were a bench up here. Maybe I could donate one so people could sit up here and look at the falls."

Wade turned to her, his face a mask of anger and pain. "You want to know what's wrong, Reese? That right there. You see a problem, and you just want to fix it by throwing money at it. Like money and buying things can fix everything."

She blinked, shocked at his vehement attack. "What are you talking about? I don't know where you got this idea that I throw money around."

He arched an eyebrow at her. "So says the girl who got twenty packages in the mail from a shopping spree and is wearing new clothes and a pair of two-hundred-dollar hiking boots."

This is what he was so upset about? The packages in the mail?

"I got *five* packages in the mail yesterday, and if you had stuck around long enough to talk, you would have seen that two of them were from my dad's secretary, Lena. I asked her to go by my apartment and send me some clothes. She's like a second mother to me and wanted to help. So, I am not wearing a *new* outfit, you just haven't seen it before. I hate to shop, and I just keep my things nice so that I don't have to."

She sighed. "I bought a couple of books on the craft of writing from a used bookstore, and I ordered a lightweight raincoat." She looked down at her feet. "As for these boots, I bought them because of *you*. You told me that you liked to hike, so I googled about hiking and everything I read said that the most important thing to have was a good pair of boots. I wanted to surprise you and suggest a hike and knew I would already be out of my element—and didn't want to add getting blisters to the mix."

His face softened. "You googled hiking? For me?" The corners of his mouth tipped up in the slightest grin. "You realize hiking is basically just walking. Except you do it outdoors. How can you mess that up?"

Shrugging her shoulders, she offered him a small smile. She might be close to breaking through and getting to the root of his anger.

She touched his hand, and this time he let it stay on top of his. "Wade, I work hard at my job, and it pays me well. I like to save, and I have money put aside because I am a cheapskate at heart and don't have enough of a social life to spend a lot of money on. If I go anywhere, it's always been with my dad or a guy like my dad who paid for everything and whose ego stood in the way of me spending any money. When I do buy things, though, I like to buy quality things that will last. Like these hiking boots."

He blew out his breath and stared across the water, not looking at her. "Listen, I'm sorry I flew off the handle. All those packages and the expensive gift you gave my grandmother just reminded me of Tawnya."

"The woman you were engaged to before?"

"Yeah, the one who acted like she loved me, then used me for my solid bank account and good credit score. I don't talk about it much, because I'm ashamed that I let myself get roped in and taken advantage of so bad, but Tawnya left me with a mountain of debt and a bruised ego. She hated that my job paid so little and that I couldn't buy her more expensive things."

What a witch. She'd wondered why Wade was so close-lipped about his ex.

He narrowed his eyes at her. "I'm well aware of the men you're used to being around, Reese. And I'm not like them. And I never will be. I can't take you to fancy clubs and expensive restaurants or buy you nice gifts."

What was he talking about?

Where had he come up with these ideas? Did he think she was like Tawnya—the money-grubbing ex he just described? Her anger flared, but she took a deep breath, trying to stay calm and understand the place of hurt that he was coming from.

"I never asked you to. I don't care about fancy restaurants. I adore our picnic lunches where we sit outside, and you sneak your crusts to my dog. You *cannot* do that in a nice restaurant. And I loved that you took me fishing. That you shared a part of yourself with me. You taught me something new."

She looked up at him with a wicked grin. "And I don't just mean that thing you do with your tongue."

He laughed and pulled her into a hug.

She breathed deep as she relaxed into his arms. This felt so good. *He* felt so good. "Can we just go back to being friends again? To having fun and fooling around with each other?"

He tipped her chin up to look at him. "Yeah, I would like that. But by fooling around, do you mean joking and flirting, or do you mean getting naked at my cottage later tonight?"

Her grin widened. She slid her hand down and in an uncharacteristic move, grabbed his butt.

A nervous giggle escaped her as she peered up at him and simply said, "Yes, that's exactly what I mean."

Chapter Eight

Reese knocked on the door of Wade's cottage, her pulse already quickening at the thought of being with him again.

Sitting through dinner tonight had been torture. She swore the man made eating pork chops look sexy.

His hand had brushed hers several times as they passed the food, and she'd squeaked a little as his foot rubbed against her bare leg in a tantalizing game of footsie.

He opened the door, and she wanted to jump him.

His hair was wet from a recent shower, and he was barefoot, wearing only a pair of faded jeans.

And, oh dear Lord, the top button was undone, as if the little silver snap were an invitation.

An invitation that she planned to RSVP to right now.

She held up a bottle of wine and two mugs that she'd snuck from the kitchen. "I don't know that Bob's Liquor down on Fourth has the most exquisite wine choices, but I did the best I could."

He looked her up and down and made a low growling sound in his throat. Pulling her to him, he laid a kiss on her, then whispered, "You are so damn beautiful."

Forget the wine. Forget everything except how quickly she could get out of her clothes. This man made her weak in the knees, and she wanted him. Now.

She scanned the one-room cottage and set the wine and cups down on the coffee table. The well-kept room was decorated in a cabin style with dark woods and bear decor.

A hint of moisture from Wade's shower and the scent of his aftershave filled the air. The room was dimly lit from the light above the sink in the small kitchenette and the canoe-shaped lamp on his bedside table.

A queen-sized bed sat in one corner of the room, and she took Wade's hand and tugged him toward it.

"Don't you want some wine?" he asked. "I probably have some real wineglasses around here."

She narrowed her eyes, going for a sexy and smoldering look. "All I want right now is you—in this bed."

Giving him a gentle push, he toppled to the bed, and she climbed on top of him, straddling his jean-clad legs.

She wanted control. She wanted to make decisions and her own choices.

Right now her choice was Wade, and she meant to control this night. To seize the power and hold him spellbound as she had her way with him.

Then she'd allow him to have his way with her.

He chuckled softly. "You're kinda bossy in bed."

"That's right. Tonight I'm the boss. And you have to do what I say and let me do whatever I want to you." She narrowed her eyes. "Is that okay with you?"

The look in his eyes went from surprised to naughty, and he grinned. "Uh, yeah. I mean, yes, totally."

Pulling off her T-shirt, she was thankful Lena had included fresh bra and panty sets in the clothes she'd sent. By the way Wade was eyeing the lacy black bra she wore, she assumed he was glad, too.

He reached up, running the backs of his fingers across the tops of her breasts, and sent a shiver of pleasure down her back. His eyes were molten, filled with liquid heat as he slowly perused her body.

"First rule is no touching until I say." Taking his hands, she drew them over his head and linked them together. "Except by me. I get to touch all I want."

His face wore a huge grin, and he looked like he'd just won the booty-call lottery. "Touch whatever you want, babe. Hell, touch things twice."

He was into it, and she had the insane urge to put on a show for him. She slowly stripped off her bra and tossed it to the floor.

Running her hands along his muscled chest, she teased and tickled and loved the soft growl that sounded from the back of his throat.

The man had amazing muscles.

He sucked in his breath as she traced the waistband of his jeans, stopping to slowly unzip the zipper.

Oh. My. Ranger Wade wasn't wearing any underwear.

She slid down his legs, pulling his jeans free and leaving him naked on the bed.

His gaze never left her as she stood and unfastened her shorts. She skimmed the fabric down her legs and stepped free of them.

Wearing only a pair of black lace thong panties, she resumed her spot, deliberately rubbing against him as she straddled his hips.

She shook out her hair, knowing that the movement jiggled her breasts as well. Wade's eyes widened, and his slow swallow gave her all the confidence she needed as she leaned forward, the tips of her nipples brushing his chest.

Nibbling and tasting, she feasted on his neck, drawing

assurance from the way his hips bucked under her. She ran her hands along his muscled arms as he gripped the dowels of the headboard.

She sat up, arching her back, and let him look at her.

His sudden hitch of breath told her he liked the show, and she reveled in the feeling of being in command of the situation. "Would you like to touch me now?"

He nodded, his gaze locked on hers. "Yes." His voice was deep, full of want.

Wade reached up and filled his hands with her breasts. A thrill of desire raced through her, and her insides tightened with need.

His hand slid up her neck, cupped her head, and pulled her down on top of him. His lips found hers, and he kissed her with a fiery passion.

Riding his hips, she moved in rhythm with their kisses, drawing moans of desire from him. Every part of her ached to touch more of him, to feel him tighter against her.

Finally allowed to touch her, his hands raced over her body—caressing, fondling.

With a growl of need, he rose up, grabbing her waist, and flipped her over. A quick movement of his hand stripped her panties down her legs, then he was on top of her, his weight a welcome pressure.

His voice, husky and raw, spoke next to her ear. "I want you, Reese. I want you now."

A soft "Yes" was all she could gasp as her legs wrapped around his waist.

A wanton need consumed her, and everything else fell away. She craved this man with a hunger she'd never felt before.

He reached for the bedside table, yanking at the drawer in his haste. Fumbling for a foil-wrapped package, he spilled the box then grabbed one from the pile. He ripped the top free and reached down, covering himself with the protection.

Her breath came in ragged gasps as she lay beneath him, in anticipation of what was to come. She pulled him down, reveling in his weight on top of her.

His fingers dug into her hair, and his breath was warm on her neck as he filled her. Slow and steady, his hips moved against hers, increasing in tempo.

He felt so damn good, so right.

He whispered her name, and she was gone. She lost all control.

But this time it was okay.

In fact, it was utterly amazing.

Chapter Nine

The next week flew by in a blur.

Working at the park in the morning, they made great progress on the little building. Too quickly.

Wade found himself wanting to take extended breaks because he wasn't ready for the project to end. Wasn't ready for Reese to leave.

They laughed and flirted as they worked, finding little ways to touch or brush against each other. She spent the afternoons back at the bed and breakfast working on her book while he tried to get his work done in the park office.

Tried was the key word.

Every time he tried to concentrate on a report or work on the schedule, his mind drifted to Reese. And his mind especially liked to drift to naked Reese.

He struggled to focus, but all he could think about was her in his bed, on the floor, or her slick and sudsy body as he'd soaped her up in the bathtub the night before.

They took their meals in the evening with Gram, talking over their day and sharing stories with Miss Abigail.

But after dinner, as the dusk settled in, they were drawn to each other like moths to a flame. And boy did they make a great flame.

That woman was going to kill him. He could not get enough of her. It was like his body knew she was only going to be around for so long, and he was taking his fill while he could.

She made him feel good. Too good.

It wouldn't last.

He knew she had to go back to Denver. Had a life somewhere else. But for now, he took what he could get. A tiny part of his mind wondered if she was using him. He knew she was on the rebound from another relationship, and he was just the Band-Aid for her hurt. But damned if he didn't enjoy being that Band-Aid.

"Can you hand me another nail?" Reese asked, drawing him from his musings. She stood on the ladder, and he took a second to admire the view of her rump at eye level. Her hip jutted out just a bit as she held a trim board in place, waiting for a nail.

He grabbed one and handed it up to her then ran his hand up her leg, stopping just short of her butt. His fingers itched to grab hold and pull her from the ladder, lay her in the grass, rip those little shorts off, and have his way with her.

"I know exactly what you're thinking," she said, as she hammered the nail in then eased down the ladder. Raking her fingers through his hair, she dropped a quick kiss on his lips and gave him a naughty grin. "Hold that thought until tonight. Then I can add a few of my ideas in as well."

He chuckled. "I do tend to like your ideas." Especially the one she'd had the night before when she'd invited him to come over to have a sundae for dessert.

His jaw had hit the floor when she'd opened her door wearing nothing but half a can of whipped cream and a couple of maraschino cherries.

"You're thinking about the whipped cream, aren't you?" She smiled slyly.

"That was a pretty good idea." He leaned in and nuzzled her neck. "What's your idea for tonight?"

"I was kind of thinking of going out."

"Out? You mean like outside? We could go back down to the lake."

She laughed. "Not that the lake isn't a great idea, but I mean out-out. Your grandmother was telling me about the Summer Festival in town. She said it starts tonight, and they're doing a chili cook-off and having a street dance."

He shrugged. "I could probably be persuaded to eat some chili. But you don't strike me as a girl that likes country music."

"You just might be surprised by a lot of things that I like, Mr. Ranger."

He grinned. "I know you like that thing I did with the whipped cream last night."

Reese giggled, and a pink blush colored her cheeks. "Yes, I did like that, too. Now hand me that two-by-four and let's get back to work. I want to finish this in time to help Miss Abigail with her chili entry. I've never actually made chili before, but I'm excited to learn. I love spicy foods."

So did he. He was finding a lot of things that he liked spicy lately. Like his new relationship with the blond-haired city girl—and the hotter the better.

. . .

Maybe this wasn't such a great idea. The Summer Festival had sounded fun but she hadn't counted on the number of people in town who were interested in Wade's sex life.

He held her hand as they walked through the booths lining the streets. The men seemed to give him nods of encouragement while the women gave her mean looks. Wade had been here the whole time. If they wanted him, why hadn't they gone after him sooner?

Evidently all it took to get him was a night of topless fishing and a can of whipped cream.

"Yoo-hoo!" a familiar voice called out. Reese was glad to see the friendly smile of Miss Abigail as she beckoned them to a picnic table.

Wade leaned in to kiss his grandmother's cheek before directing her to the opposite bench seat.

Rows of tables sat in the street in a semi-circle around a large open area for dancing. The band was warming up on the stage as they sat down. "Wow, there's quite a turnout for this event."

Miss Abigail nodded. "Oh yes, this is one of the favorites amongst the locals. Everybody loves to kick up their heels and do a little street dancing." She gestured to the older man sitting next to her. "This is Harry Langston. He's the owner of the Cotton Creek Gazette and my special friend for the night."

Hmmm. Did *special friend* mean he was her date or that they planned to get jiggy with it later on?

Either way—ewww!

"Nice to meet you, Mr. Langston. I'm Reese Hudson." She smiled and shook his hand, trying to get the image of him and Miss Abigail out of her mind.

"I like your dress, honey," Miss Abigail said.

Nothing she had would have been suitable for the street dance, so she'd snuck into town earlier that afternoon to Cotton Creek's one dress shop. She'd found a white pair of wedge sandals and a simple summer dress in a gorgeous shade of pink. Its A-line style and slim shoulder straps were a great fit for her figure.

The neckline was a little low, but she had the bust to fill

it, and she'd enjoyed Wade's sexy-eyed look of approval when she'd opened the door of her room earlier that night.

"I like your dress," he'd said in a sexy slow drawl. "But I'd like it better on the floor."

The steamy kiss he'd given her next was almost enough to have them call off going to the dance and stay home instead.

The band piped up with a slow country song, and Wade slid out of the bench seat. "The first dance always goes to my best gal." Before Reese could reply, he turned to his grandmother and held out his hand. "Gram, may I have this dance?"

Miss Abigail laughed and winked at Reese. "Isn't he just the sweetest boy?" She took Wade's hand. "I hope I can trust you to keep an eye on Mr. Langston. He's quite a catch, you know?"

Reese smiled at Mr. Langston as he gave her a dashing grin. With his balding head of white hair and short stature, she wasn't sure what made him such a catch, but maybe older gentlemen with all their teeth were in short supply in Cotton Creek.

"Would you care to dance, Ms. Hudson?" he asked.

She shook her head. "Oh no, I'm not much of a dancer. And please call me Reese."

"Then you must call me Harry." He slid from the seat and held out his arm. "And I won't take no for an answer."

She hadn't realized quite how short he was until she stood up next to him in the wedge sandals. He led her to the dance floor and when she turned to him she realized that his nose was at the exact level of her cleavage.

The tips of his ears turned as pink as her dress as he drew his eyes up from her boobs to her face.

Oh boy. This was going to be a long dance.

Fortunately, Harry was a skilled dancer and led her deftly around the dance floor. Country music had never been her thing, and she tried to keep up with Harry's footwork, stumbling a few times and stepping on the poor man's feet.

He was a kind-hearted man and patient with her as he taught her the dance and held a conversation at the same time. Obviously Miss Abigail had told him why she was in town, and he asked about the progress at the park and how her writing was going.

It was a secret thrill to have someone treat her like a real writer, and she gushed about the story she was currently working on while she tried to keep up with the steps.

"It sounds like it has an interesting premise. Would you like me to take a look at it? Offer you some tips?" Harry asked.

"Yes, I'd love that."

"Why don't you come down to the paper later this week? I've got some contacts in the publishing world, and I can look over your work and give you some names of a few people to contact when you're ready. And I'm always looking for some good news stories if you want to try your hand at writing a few articles for the local paper."

She couldn't believe her luck. Getting advice from a seasoned writer like Harry could be a huge help to her. "Thank you. And I'll start thinking of some ideas for articles."

The song ended, and a new faster-paced song began. Undaunted, Harry grabbed her hand and attempted to teach her how to swing dance.

Feeling like an awkward goose next to a graceful swan, she valiantly tried to keep up with the swinging and twirling.

Her head was taller than Harry's reach, and the last whirl sent her careening into the table filled with drinks. A stack of plastic cups toppled over and rolled into the street.

"So sorry," she said to the teenage girl manning the drink table. Her hip aching from the bump against the table, she tried to retreat from the dance area.

But Mr. Langston was determined to teach her to swing, and he tugged her back into his arms. He smelled like a cross between breath mints and Ben-Gay, and he laughed easily over her mishap. She had to admire his tenacity and positive spirit.

Before another embarrassing mishap, a deep voice spoke from over her shoulder. "Can I cut in?"

Her heart skipped a beat as Wade stepped in and wrapped a muscled arm around her waist. Thank goodness.

Saved by the ranger.

Pulling her close, he moved her smoothly across the dance floor, keeping perfect rhythm with the song.

In Wade's arms, she transformed into a nimble dancer.

Okay, maybe not transformed, but at least she could keep up and wasn't swinging into unsuspecting punch bowls. She sighed and relaxed into the dance.

He was so wonderfully tall, and she laid her head against his shoulder and inhaled his manly scent. He smelled so good, and she felt so right in his arms.

Dang. She was in trouble.

Her heart bounced around in her chest, and she couldn't stop smiling. They had less than a day's work left on their project, then there'd be no reason to stay in town. But she wasn't ready to say good-bye to the ranger.

She needed to tell Wade she was leaving this weekend. Best to make it quick. Rip it off like a Band-Aid. Act like it's no big deal. It's not like he was emotionally invested, either. He would probably be glad to get her and Bagel out of his hair.

Yes, that was the smart choice. Tell him tonight.

But first, she could enjoy this dance—this night. Revel in the feel of his arms around her as he glided them along the dance floor.

A thin sliver of pleasure ran down her spine as he softly

sang the lyrics to the sweet country song into her ear.

His voice was low and husky, and her insides warmed as she thought about a different kind of dance she wanted to do with him. A dance that involved just the two of them, alone in a room, with the same country song, but a lot less clothes.

She would tell him she was leaving. Soon. Maybe just not right now.

And just maybe he would ask her to stay.

• • •

Wade drew Reese close to him as he two-stepped her across the dance floor. She was a good dancer and fit perfectly in his arms.

Everything was perfect about her tonight. From the way her long blond hair fell in loose curls around her bare shoulders to the way she filled out that pink dress.

Damn, did she ever fill out that dress. Or mostly fill out.

Unfortunately, he wasn't the only man at the street dance who'd noticed how amazing Reese looked, and he'd experienced little nigglings of unease as he'd watched the guys from the park give her appreciative once-overs.

He knew those guys and was sure the thoughts going with those looks were not rated G.

He'd kept Reese by his side most of the night, but damned if Toby from maintenance hadn't asked her to dance the minute he'd stepped away to grab them a couple of beers.

What was wrong with him? Reese didn't belong to him. She could dance with whoever she wanted to.

Hold up now.

He took a step forward as Toby's hand inched lower on Reese's waist. His coworker looked up and caught his eye, and the meaning behind it, and quickly moved his hand back up.

Jealousy spiked, taking him by surprise. He wasn't the jealous type. Or he hadn't been until now.

What made her different? And what did it matter? She'd be gone in a few days anyway.

Maybe he could ask her to stay. Just to spend the weekend or a few more days.

Maybe he could draw the project out, make it take a little longer.

Who was he kidding?

Reese had a life in Denver. A job, friends, her dad. She wasn't going to want to stay up here in this Podunk town when she had a future waiting for her in Denver.

What could he offer her anyway? A busted down pickup and a mountain of credit card debt. Didn't sound like much of an offer to him.

Reese was used to flashy cars and eating in expensive restaurants. He preferred his grandmother's home-cooked meals to anything that was offered in a fancy restaurant. She played tennis in a country club while he liked to go fishing on a lake or hike into the mountains.

They were just too different. And he didn't need all the extra complications Reese Hudson and her chubby little pug would bring.

Probably better that she was leaving. It would make things easier on them both.

Besides, it wasn't like she was emotionally invested or anything. She'd probably be glad to get him out of her hair.

Oh great. Now he was thinking about her hair. The way it felt like silk as it ran through his fingers. The way it fell across his pillow as she lay under him in bed. And the way it smelled.

Lord have mercy, her hair smelled amazing.

"Did you get one of those beers for me?" Reese stood in front of him, her question breaking through his thoughts. She smiled up at him, her face happy and lit like a ray of sunshine.

He handed her a bottle, and her fingers brushed his as she took it. "I saw Toby trying to grab your ass as you danced."

Geez. Where did that come from? He'd planned to say something about getting her a cold one, but it seemed her happy positive vibe somehow brought out his dark thoughts of jealousy and her leaving.

Her smile fell and her happy expression was replaced with one of surprise. "What's wrong? Are you jealous?" The smile returned, this time taking over her whole face. "You are. You got jealous that someone else was dancing with me."

He could feel his own scowl deepen. "Why does that make you so durned happy?" He would never understand women.

She leaned forward, putting her lips next to his ear and inadvertently giving him a great view down the front of her dress. His face might be scowling, but other parts of him were suddenly feeling very happy as her breath tickled his neck.

"That means you like me," she whispered, her voice low and sexy.

Yes. He guessed that's exactly what it meant.

But she didn't need to know that. "Don't get cocky. Maybe I just don't want half the town looking down your dress or trying to cop a feel."

She grinned up at him. "Because you like me."

The smile happened before he could stop it. He felt the corner of his lip twitch upward, and he took a swig of beer to hide the expression.

Too late. She saw it and grinned back.

Her grin turned impish, and he knew a naughty thought had just crossed her mind. "How about you take me back to your place, and I let you look down my dress *and* cop a feel. Or two."

"Or ten." He did like the way this woman thought. Grabbing her hand, he waved good-bye to his grandmother and Harry and tugged her toward the truck. "Let's go."

· · ·

The following Monday morning Wade stepped out of his truck. He carried a tray of iced coffees and a bag of maple-iced donuts.

Reese was already on the job site, her blond hair pulled up into a ponytail and a blue ball cap on her head. She wore the khaki shorts that he loved and a tank top that clung to all the right spots.

Damn. This was a view he'd miss.

The project was almost finished. It wouldn't take them more than another day or two. That thought didn't make him happy.

"What's this?" Reese asked, taking the tray of coffees from him.

"Iced coffee. I had them put in cream and the flavor you like." He drew an arm across his forehead. "It's too hot for regular coffee."

"I've never had an iced coffee. I've always wanted to try one." She pursed her lips around the straw and took a sip. He couldn't help but look at her mouth. She had a great mouth.

She closed her eyes in bliss. How come everything she did seemed sexy as hell to him?

"Yum. It's delicious." She opened her eyes and grinned at him. "I love it when you introduce me to new things."

"You mean like that thing last night in the truck?"

She laughed. "Well, yes, that, but I also meant like fishing, and frog legs, and maple-iced donuts." She eyed the bag he was holding. "Speaking of which, do you by any chance have my new favorite flavor in that bag?"

"I sure do." He passed her the bag, not sure if he could take watching her eat a donut.

He loved the way she licked the frosting from her lips.

Dang. He had it bad.

What would he do next week when she was gone?

He had started to look forward to seeing her every day. Counted on hearing her laugh and her stupid jokes.

Maybe he should tell her how he felt. Tell her that she meant something to him and that he wasn't ready for her to go back to the city and leave him behind.

He could suggest that maybe they both take a week of vacation. Go backpacking in the mountains. Get to know each other better. Nothing helps you to know the real personality of a woman until you take her into the mountains for a few days with only a backpack.

Somehow he thought Reese would do fine.

He imagined her laughing and taking everything in stride. Finding the positive in all of their experiences.

Or maybe he could ask her to go away with him. They could drive down to Santa Fe, or he could take her to Mesa Verde.

Yeah. Right. With what?

He couldn't afford to take a week's vacation and with all the debt Tawnya left him, he couldn't afford to pay for a weekend in a hotel, let alone a whole week.

Who was he kidding? Even without the credit card debt, he wouldn't be able to take her to the kind of hotel she was used to. He'd never be able to take her anywhere in the style she was accustomed to.

Maybe it was for the best that she was leaving. Then he could just put her out of his mind and get on with his life. Forget about her and just focus on his job and all the things he'd been letting slide at the B&B these last few weeks. Let her get back to her own life.

Uh-huh, he should just forget about her. Yeah, right.

"You all right?" Reese gave him a questioning look. She had a dab of maple glaze right above her lip, and he ached to lick it from her mouth.

Just tell her how you feel. See if there's a chance she's feeling the same way. "Yeah, sure. I was just thinking there was something I wanted to talk to you about."

There, he'd said something. Laid the groundwork. Now to actually tell her what he was feeling.

"Oh good, I need to talk to you, too. I wanted to tell you that I'm leaving on Wednesday. The building is almost done, and my dad's pressuring me to get back to work."

Wednesday?

He'd thought he would at least have the rest of the week. And he'd hoped through the weekend.

Maybe he could stall the project. Add in an extra task they needed to complete. "Oh yeah, of course. I understand."

She picked up a paintbrush. "I thought since we were down to the painting, we'd be able to finish up today or tomorrow. Is that right, or do you think it will take longer?"

Yes. It will take much longer. Like another week. Actually another month. You need to stay.

"Nope, if we put in a good couple of days, we should be able to finish up by tomorrow and get you on the road by Wednesday. You can be back in your skirt and high heels and sitting at your desk by Thursday morning."

She frowned. "Somehow that thought doesn't excite me. I'd rather be here, painting an outhouse with you. What does that say about my life?"

She just handed out the perfect opening. *Tell her to stay, you idiot.* But the words wouldn't come. He'd somehow lost the ability to open his mouth. He shrugged.

"You said you wanted to talk to me?"

Did her face have a hint of hopefulness about it? Was she waiting for him to ask her to stay?

"Oh, uh, it was nothing, really. Just that I thought you missed a spot on the trim." He fumbled for the words to say. "And, uh, Gram wanted me to tell you to be sure to remind her about that recipe you wanted for the chocolate chip muffins."

Idiot.

"Oh, of course. I really did like those muffins." She turned the paintbrush over in her hands, and he thought he saw a tinge of pink creeping up her neck.

"I was thinking…" She hesitated. "Actually, I was wondering, if you might want to come down to Denver next weekend and go out on a date. With me, I mean."

"Um, yeah, sure, okay." Why did all of his responses make him sound like a bumbling fool? "How about Saturday night? Would that work? Pick you up at six?"

"Make it five." She grinned.

"It's a date."

"Yeah. It's a date."

• • •

Reese set the paintbrush down on top of the paint can and stood back to look at the little building.

It was done. She couldn't believe they'd finished it.

She never would have thought she could build an outhouse, and she smiled at their completed project.

Having the building finished was bittersweet though because that meant she wouldn't see Wade every day anymore.

Wouldn't get to start her day eating donuts and drinking coffee with him, wouldn't get to brush up against him as they worked side by side, wouldn't get to sneak up to the waterfall and kiss in front of the rushing water.

It was late afternoon on Tuesday, and she wished she hadn't decided to go home on Wednesday. She wanted one more day. Hell, she wanted one more week—one more month—to spend with him.

"Nice work," Wade said, walking past her to load his tools into the truck. "I'm proud of you."

Her chest filled with pride. "Thanks. I'm kind of proud of me, too. I never thought I'd be able to do this."

He grinned down at her. "You've done a lot of new things these past few weeks."

A warm flush crept up her neck. "How do you know I haven't tried some of those things before?"

He laughed. "I meant the writing and working on the novel."

"Oh yeah, that's what I meant, too." She laughed with him.

"By the way, I read the new pages you gave me yesterday, and I thought they were great. I really like the plot line and where you're taking the story. You really drew me in to the new scene, and I cracked up at that part where she told her boss to take a hike."

The satisfaction she felt in completing the outhouse didn't begin to compare to the pride she felt at Wade's words of encouragement about her writing.

She'd been surprised when he'd offered to read some of her work and even more shocked when he'd actually read it and offered constructive criticism. She loved talking over the plot of the book with him. He was a great sounding board, as he listened and threw out new ideas. His encouragement gave her the confidence to keep going and filled her heart with deeper feelings for him.

"Thanks. I had a lot of fun writing that part."

"I bet." He set his tool box in the backseat of the truck and pulled out a package of toilet paper. "Here's the last piece to finishing the outhouse. You want to do the final honors?"

"Sure."

He tossed her the package, and she opened the door to the little building. A plexi-glass skylight offered plenty of light as the door shut behind her. She filled the holder with a fresh roll and put the rest of the package into the small cabinet

Wade had built for supplies.

The little room smelled like sawdust and fresh paint. She looked around, happy and proud of what they'd created.

On a whim, she pulled a Sharpie marker from her tool pouch. Inside the cabinet, on an inconspicuous wall, she drew a heart and wrote "*WB + RH*" inside.

It was silly and juvenile, but also seemed fitting and somehow wildly romantic.

If Wade saw it, he'd probably tease her about defacing park property. But she didn't care.

She'd left her mark on this building by drawing the heart. Hopefully she'd left her mark on the actual heart of the man whose initials she'd just written.

. . .

Wednesday came way too fast for Wade.

He carried Reese's things down to her car and stood waiting while she said good-bye to his grandmother. Gram would have no trouble asking her to stay a little longer or to come back for a visit.

In fact, the reason Reese was leaving mid-afternoon was because Gram had talked her into staying for lunch. And dessert.

The screen door slammed, and Reese walked out, the chunky little pug in her arms.

He was going to miss that funny little mutt, too. With all the pampering Reese and Gram had given it, the dog's leg had healed, and it was getting around fine now.

He reached for the dog and held him against his chest. "Take it easy, Bagel. Stay off that leg." He smiled at Reese. "I know it sounds funny, but I'm going to miss this guy."

A sad look crossed her face before she quickly replaced it with a smile. "He's going to miss you, too. He's gotten used to all the attention and affection."

Was she still talking about the dog? "Well, keep up the writing."

Her smile turned into a full-faced grin. "Oh, I will. I've already completed half the book, and I can't wait to finish it. I think about it all the time." She gave him a naughty smile. "Well, not *all* the time."

He chuckled. "Keep me in mind if you need to work on any of those bedroom scenes. I can help you work out where your hero might put his hands. Or his lips."

She grinned up at him. "Bedroom scenes? Don't you mean scenes at the lake, and on the hiking trails, and in a truck?"

He grinned back. "Yeah, I can help you with those, too."

He loved how they could so easily banter back and forth. She made him laugh like no one else did. And he loved how she looked so classy and then let dirty little jokes fall out of her mouth.

He wanted to take her in his arms and give her a proper good-bye.

Better yet, tell her to stay. Just a few more days.

"I bet your clients will be happy to see you."

She set her purse in the front seat and reached for the dog. "Oh shoot, that reminds me. My dad planned a big thing with a couple of our clients for Saturday night. There's no way I can get out of it. Would you be okay if we moved our date out one week and you came down the next weekend?"

His smile faltered.

Was this how it was going to be? Was this her subtle way of getting rid of him? Just keep putting him off until he went away?

Bagel whined and licked his face as she took the dog from his arms.

"Sure, that's fine."

She set the dog in the passenger seat and turned back to him. Raising her arms, she linked them around his neck. "I'm really sorry. I could try to get out of it. I could start faking a cough now." Her eyes shone with amusement, and she feigned a quick little cough.

"Nah, it's okay. I've got stuff to do this weekend anyway." Pulling her against him, he leaned down and kissed her gently.

She pressed into him, deepening the kiss, sliding her tongue between his lips and ravaging his mouth.

His hands slid down and cupped her butt. Her luscious round ass fit perfectly into his palms. She fit perfectly against him. Like she was the missing puzzle piece that would complete his life.

He didn't want her to go. He wanted to keep kissing her—touching her. He wanted to lay her down on the hood of that very expensive car and make her engine purr.

She drew back, her breath ragged and her eyes bright. "I've got to go. But I will see you in a week and a half. And Wade"—she dipped her chin and looked up at him through her long dark eyelashes—"make sure you bring your pajamas and a toothbrush."

She pulled away and climbed into her car.

Shutting the door, she spoke to him through the open window. "On second thought, forget the pajamas. Just bring the toothbrush." She winked and put the car into gear.

He chuckled. "Got it."

"See you next week." She waved and pulled away.

He watched her car drive down the long driveway and turn onto the highway.

A heavy weight filled his gut, and he dismissed the idea that he could be missing her already.

This was no big deal. They'd see each other in a few days.

So why did it feel so final? Like this was the end of something. Something good.

Something he didn't want to let go of.

Okay, so he hadn't asked her to stay. But at least he knew he would see her again. That was something.

But now they would be on her home turf. She'd have home field advantage.

What if this was really just a test to see if he could hack it in her world?

Chapter Ten

The doorbell rang.

Her mouth went dry, and her pulse quickened as she tried not to run for the front door of her apartment.

She'd been thinking about this night all week and had everything planned.

They would start with dinner at a fun Irish pub downtown that served the best fish and chips in town, then head out to the sports field where she had tickets to a professional soccer game. The fans were rowdy, and she'd reserved great seats right by the field.

She couldn't wait to surprise Wade.

She wore jeans, cute sandals, and a gorgeous emerald green sleeveless top that brought out the green in her eyes.

He'd told her once that he loved the color of her eyes. That they reminded him of the water in the lake.

Maybe that might not sound too romantic to some, but it reminded her of their night at the lake, and she got a little shiver of delight just thinking about it.

Checking her hair once more in the mirror as she walked

by—she'd worn it loose and curled—she took a deep breath and opened the door.

Surprise.

The sight of Wade took her breath away. He was gorgeous.

But the surprise was on her as he stood at her doorstep holding a single pink flower and wearing a suit and tie.

His black suit fit him in all the right places, and the way he smiled at her sent little tingles of pleasure coursing through her.

Suddenly shy, she hesitated, not sure if she should hug him or throw him down in the hall and jump him right there. "Hi."

Saving her, he leaned forward and pulled her into his arms. "Hi, yourself. You look great."

He *felt* great. So solid and warm. And he smelled amazing.

She wanted to forget going out and just drag him into her bedroom and spend the weekend naked in bed. "Thanks. Come on in."

She stepped back and let him in to the apartment. His good-natured smile fell as he appeared to take in the opulent apartment.

To her, it was just her place, but she suddenly saw her apartment from new eyes. From his eyes.

It probably did seem a little posh. Her dad had hired a decorator, and she'd let him, of course. She never felt that she needed such an elegant place and sometimes felt afraid to make a mess.

Her apartment was a beautiful mix of contemporary and chic. Decorated in cool hues, shades of blue and green dotted the room in the form of throw pillows and artwork. Thick rugs covered gleaming hardwood floors, and a large watercolor painting covered one wall.

The apartment was set up in a great-room arrangement with the kitchen and living area as one big room separated by a large island. The black countertops gleamed, and the room smelled like the vanilla scented candle that burned there.

Her kitchen was spotless, not because she loved to clean, but because she never cooked. She was terrible in the kitchen and had her three favorite takeout restaurants on speed-dial.

The apartment stayed neat due to her dad's insistence on paying for a cleaning service once a week. She felt so bad that someone had to clean up after her, that she often cleaned the apartment the night before they arrived. They'd been a godsend this last week, though, as she'd come home from work every night and delved into her manuscript.

Thoughts of her story filled her head as she worked, and she couldn't wait to get home each night and fill the pages with her ideas.

She'd been dying to tell Wade all about her latest thoughts about the storyline.

Except now she seemed shy, almost embarrassed at the richness of her apartment as she watched Wade eyeball the size of the flat-screen plasma television affixed to the wall.

He whistled as he took in the rooms and tugged uncomfortably at his tie. "Pretty swanky place you got here."

She shrugged. "It's okay. My dad brought someone in to decorate. Personally I love the shabby chic feel of the bed and breakfast more."

He raised a questioning eyebrow at her. "Yeah, I bet you do."

He handed her the flower. "This is for you. Gram told me to pick the prettiest flower in her garden for you." He reached into his suit jacket pocket and pulled out a slim rawhide. "And this is for Bagel."

Awww. He'd handpicked a flower for her and brought a gift for her dog.

Her heart melted.

Wade looked around. "Where is the little guy?"

"I left him at my dad's for the night since I didn't know how late we'd be staying out."

Although now all she could think about was how soon they'd be getting in. To bed.

Wade eyed her outfit. "Am I early? Did I not give you enough time to change?"

"No, you're great. You're right on time. I just got off work late. It won't take me but a few minutes to change." She pointed to the fridge. "Grab yourself something to drink. I'll be right back."

Shutting the door of her bedroom, she shimmied out of her clothes as she scrambled for a new plan for the evening.

Who knew Wade would show up in a suit? She was expecting his normal jeans and cowboy boots.

Not that she was complaining.

Ranger Wade could rock the hell out of a suit.

She scanned her closet and grabbed a turquoise blue summer dress, a short cotton number that hugged her figure. It was a little sexier style than she normally wore, but she'd bought it on a whim last week when she'd seen it at the mall.

Throwing caution to the wind, she stripped off her bra and shimmied the girls into the halter-style top of the dress.

She was probably a little too busty to go braless with this dress, especially with its deep plunging neckline, but hey, this was the new Reese. The one who didn't conform, who dated park rangers and went out to dinner without a bra.

Sliding her feet into a pair of strappy high heels, she fluffed out her hair and was glad she'd decided to wear it down and loose.

"Okay, I'm ready." She stepped out of her room, a little nervous about her bold wardrobe choice.

Brock would never let her wear anything that even hinted at sexy. He wanted her looking respectable and chaste. Like a good country club girl.

Respectable and chaste could take a hike.

She had the figure to wear something sexy, and she'd enjoyed the last few weeks in Cotton Creek where she could dress however she wanted. She'd had fun wearing her clothes a little more on the racy side as she'd tried to win over the ranger.

But this was the city, and they were going out.

She looked up at Wade and was rewarded with a wide-eyed ogle.

His eyes roamed from her bare legs to her eye-popping cleavage, and his Adam's apple bobbed in his throat as he swallowed. "Wow. You look amazing. I'm not sure it's safe for you to go out like that. You could stop traffic in that dress."

She loved the way he eyed her, not with scorn for not dressing proper enough, but with a greedy look of hunger like he wanted to devour her.

He casually leaned against the counter, holding a can of orange soda, and she had a fleeting thought of how easy it would be for Wade to peel off her dress and take her against those spotless kitchen counters.

A blush crept up her cheeks, and he grinned as if he read her mind.

She swallowed and grabbed her purse, knowing that if they didn't leave now, her willpower would crumble, and they wouldn't make it out of her kitchen.

The lone pink flower sat by the sink in a tumbler full of water, and a goofy grin crept across her face at the touching gesture of Wade picking out a flower for her. "Thanks for the flower. I love it."

He hoisted the can up and offered her an easy smile. "Thanks for the orange soda. It's my favorite."

"I know. That's why I got it. I paid attention to what you like."

His smile turned naughty, and he drawled, "You do a lot

of things that I like."

Her insides did a little tumble at the way he smiled at her, and his deep, low voice swirled around her like a warm cloak.

She loved that she knew one of his favorite things and that he'd noticed and thanked her. Unlike Brock, who'd expected her to detail and catalogue all of his wants and needs.

It was much more fun to surprise someone with a thoughtful gesture than be expected to do one.

In fact, just about everything seemed more fun with Wade. And she couldn't wait to start their date.

Actually, she couldn't wait to end their date, in her bed.

Before another blush could grab her, she reached for her scarf and busied herself with arranging it around her shoulders. "We should probably head out. Where did you park?"

Wade left his soda can on the counter and sidled over to her. Yeah, even in the suit, he still had the swagger of a man used to wearing cowboy boots. "I'm in the lot down the street."

"We should probably take my car then. You may never find another spot later tonight." She pushed the intercom button next to her front door. "Don, will you have someone bring my car up? We're going out to dinner this evening."

A man's clipped voice responded. "Of course, Ms. Hudson, right away."

Wade raised an eyebrow, but said nothing as they exited her apartment and headed for the elevator. The car was empty, and Wade placed a hand on the small of her back to guide her into the small space.

The warmth of his hand against her back sent a delicious shiver through her, and her inner minx came alive.

She tipped her head up and gave him her best seductive look. "You know you haven't kissed me hello yet."

A surprised look crossed Wade's face, followed by a

wicked grin. "Then I should remedy that right now."

He took a step closer, pressing her back against the elevator wall, and slid his hand behind her neck. Drawing her face up, he leaned in and took her mouth in a soft kiss, his lips barely grazing her.

She sighed against his mouth, tasting the faint lingering of orange soda, her fingers digging in to his shoulders.

His second kiss was deeper as he pressed into her, his lean body hard against hers as he took her mouth in a carnal onslaught of fever and lust. His hand slid down her waist, over her hip, and grabbed her butt, lifting her leg and wrapping it around him.

She pulled him to her, matching his frenzied desire as everything in her burned with heat and a passionate need.

Moaning into his mouth, she rubbed against him, desperate to feel his hands on every inch of her.

The ding of the elevator brought her back to reality.

Wade stepped back, leaving her gasping for breath and aching for his touch.

Cool and composed, he grinned down at her as the elevator doors slid open. "Hello."

Holy freaking hot hellos.

He took her hand, and she followed him out of the elevator, reeling from their passionate embrace.

The garage attendant standing by her car arched an eyebrow at her, but instead of shamefully hiding her face, she pushed back her shoulders, grinned, and acted as if it was a normal everyday occurrence for her to be ravaged in the one minute elevator ride. "Thanks for bringing my car up."

She looked over at Wade. "You want to drive?"

He shrugged. "Sure."

She leaned toward the attendant as he opened the door of her car, keeping her voice low. "Can you please call over to The Blue Bistro and reserve us a table? We're headed there now."

He nodded. "Of course, Ms. Hudson. I'll take care of it right away. Have a nice evening."

Wade rolled his eyes as she slid into the leather seat next to him. "Geez, your family must be a little more important than you let on. Everybody treats you like royalty around here."

She waved a hand at him. "Oh, it has nothing to do with me. They get paid to act that way."

He answered her with an "uh-huh" sound and put the car in gear, but his light demeanor seemed to have changed a bit.

She let the conversation drop and instead focused on giving him directions to the restaurant.

· · ·

Dang.

He could never remember if you started from the outside and went in or the inside and went out. Who needed this many dang forks anyway?

Wade adjusted the collar of his shirt, hating the constricting feeling of the tie, and waited to see which fork Reese would pick up first.

The restaurant she'd brought him to had more utensils and dishes on the table than in all of Gram's china closet. He didn't know what to do with half of this stuff.

He followed Reese's examples through most of the meal, missing half of what she said to him as he concentrated on proper etiquette and not letting steak juice drip onto his shirt.

He'd thought wearing the suit would impress her. But all it had accomplished was making him feel like a fool and reminding him he was completely out of his element.

The grandeur of her apartment had kept him from even sitting on the sofa. At least it held pieces of her charm in the little knick-knacks and funny throw pillows.

But this restaurant was something else entirely.

There were no prices on the menu and half of it was in French. At least he thought it was French. It could have been Greek or Russian for all he knew. And everything was *à* la carte.

Reese had to explain to him that when you ordered the steak, all you got was the steak, and you had to order the potatoes and salad separately.

What kind of nonsense was that?

He knew the restaurant was expensive and the steak he'd ordered would cost him a bundle. But for those prices, they couldn't throw in a baked potato or some lettuce?

They finished their meal, and he excused himself to find the restroom.

He pushed open the heavy oak door marked "Gentlemen" and stepped into an opulent room with marble floors and gleaming gold faucets on the sinks. There were no tacky urinals, but instead individual rooms with louvered oak doors.

A man wearing a dark suit stood at the sink and greeted him with a smile. "Good evening, sir. Is there anything I can help you with?"

Huh? Wade dipped his head to the man. "No thanks. I'm pretty sure I've got this under control."

He took care of business and returned to the sinks to wash his hands, all under the watchful eye of the man in the suit.

He handed Wade a towel. "Can I offer the gentleman some mouthwash or a mint?"

"Mouthwash? Do I need some?" Wade huffed a breath into his hand and sniffed.

"No, of course not, sir. No offense intended. It's just a courtesy of the restaurant." He took the wet towel from Wade and dropped it into the hamper under the counter.

"Okay, sure. Why not?"

He poured a dab of green liquid into a small disposable cup and handed it to Wade who took it, rinsed and spit before handing it back.

The man smiled and waited patiently. "Will there be anything else, sir?"

Realizing he was waiting for a tip, Wade pulled out his wallet. How much should he tip for the use of a towel and a swallow of Scope? He considered a few singles then grabbed a fiver and passed it to the mouthwash guy. "Nope, that should do it. Thanks."

He escaped the restroom before the guy offered to iron his shirt. That was for sure the most expensive mouthwash he'd ever had.

Heading back to the table, he saw a tall distinguished man standing at the table talking to Reese.

The man held out his hand and gave him an appraising glance. "You must be Wade. It's good to meet you. I'm Robert Hudson, Reese's father."

"Nice to meet you, sir. I've heard a lot about you."

Robert raised an eyebrow, and Wade thought he held the handshake just a beat too long, his grip solid and full of confidence. "I'll bet she has. But she hasn't told me much about you, Mr. Baker. Except that you work for the Forest Service."

Wade nodded, not sure if he should remain standing or resume his seat across from Reese. "Actually I work for the Park Service, sir. I've been with them for eight years now."

"What kind of degree do you need for that kind of work? Or do you just need to be in good with Smokey the Bear?"

"Dad, stop it." Reese's voice was taut.

Wade was used to these kinds of insults about his job and waved away Reese's concerns. "It's okay, Reese. Actually, I have a bachelor of science degree in park and rec administration."

Reese's dad laughed in a slightly mocking way. "I didn't know they handed out degrees in recreation."

Reese pushed back her chair and stood. "Dad, that's enough. No one handed Wade a degree. He earned it. And you seemed to have missed the administration part." She looked around for the waiter. "It was good to see you, but we were just leaving. As soon as we get our check."

Robert waved a hand in dismissal. "Oh don't worry about that. I'll take care of it. You two kids go have fun on your date."

Wade took a step forward. He was quickly losing control of this situation. "No, I couldn't let you do that, sir."

"It's already done." His tone was light, but Wade detected a whiff of condescension. "You just take care of my little girl." He leaned down and dropped a quick peck on Reese's cheek then winked at Wade. "She's my most valuable treasure. Make sure you get her home at a decent hour."

"Oh, for heaven's sake, Dad. We're leaving." She stepped around her father and grabbed Wade's hand, tugging him away from the table before he could do anything more than wave.

"Nice to meet you, sir," he called as Reese pulled him toward the door.

The warm night air hit him as they stepped outside, and he realized he was sweating. Like a nervous teenager meeting a girl's parents on their first date.

Actually, it felt more like the anxiety at a job interview.

He looked down at Reese with a grimace. "Well, that was awkward."

A pink blush deepened on Reese's cheeks. "Oh my gosh, I know. I'm so sorry. I can't believe we ran into him. I'm so embarrassed."

Yeah, that was quite a coincidence.

He figured the doorman at Reese's apartment had probably tipped him off. "You don't need to be embarrassed. I'm the one that looked like a fool. I could have paid for our meal, you know."

Her cheeks darkened further. "I know. I know. I'm sorry. But I also know how my father gets, and it would've been worse if we'd argued about it, and he'd have ended up insisting and paying for it anyway." She squeezed his hand. "Can we please try to forget this part of our evening and get back to our date?"

He looked down at her upturned face and softened at the look of pleading in her eyes. "Yeah, all right. Did you have something else planned?" He glanced at the door to the expensive restaurant. "Maybe something a little less uptight?"

She offered him a relieved smile. "Yes, of course. How about if we go listen to some music? There's a fun little Irish pub downtown that usually has a live band. It's only a few blocks from here. We could walk off our meal and go check it out."

Wade nodded. "Okay, that sounds all right. And I could use the walk."

They fell into step next to each other as they walked down the block and turned into the downtown area of Denver. Several clubs were housed in this area, and a long line of people snaked down the sidewalk in front of one.

Wade gawked at the sheer number of women lining the sidewalk, all of them dressed to the nines in heels and skimpy dresses. He'd never seen so much cleavage in one place before.

They walked along the sidewalk next to the line. "What are they all waiting for? Is a big-name band playing there tonight?"

Reese laughed. "No. Just a DJ. They're all waiting to get in. That's The High Rise, one of the most popular dance clubs downtown. They only let so many people go in, and the bouncers check out the line and only allow the best-looking inside."

"You're kidding, right? All these gorgeous women are standing in line like cattle at auction hoping a couple of meatheads will decide if they look good enough?"

"Yep. Either that or they pay big bucks to get in. It's a stupid status thing. And it's not even that great of a club. It's loud and way too crowded."

He gave her a sideways glance. "So, you've come down here and subjected yourself to this? And it sounds like you've been among the chosen ones that they let inside?"

It sounded to him like a great place to avoid.

She shrugged.

"Reeeeessseee!!!" A high-pitched shrill voice screamed her name, and two women from the line stepped out and threw themselves at Reese. One was blond and the other a brunette, and both wore short dresses and spiked high heels.

The blonde was the bearer of the shrill voice, and her words tumbled out in an exaggerated mixture of fakeness and too many shots. "Oh my gawwwdd! I'm so glad to see you. We've been waiting here forever. Your hair looks gorgeous. I just love the dress."

The brunette gave her more of an air-hug then stepped back, giving off an air of importance and confident standoffishness. She looked down her nose at Wade. "Who's your friend?"

A wave of hairspray and perfume surrounded him as the blonde flung herself at him, wrapping her arms around his neck and pressing her chest against him.

Her cleavage was blatantly on display as her breasts practically exploded out of her low-cut red dress, reminding Wade of the dough that popped out of a biscuit can when it was cracked open.

He tried not to look.

She rubbed herself against him, twisting her long nails into his hair. "You're cute."

She giggled at Reese. "Your friend is too cute, Reese. I just want to eat him up." She tilted her head up to Wade and ran her tongue along her heavily glossed lips. "Did you hear that? I just want to Eat. You. Up."

He heard all right. Reaching for her arms, he tried to pull them from around his neck and escape her grasp.

He looked to Reese for a little help, but she was being dragged to the front of the line by Ms. Snotty. He followed along, Red Dress deflecting his attempts to free himself and clinging to him like a little monkey.

They reached the two bouncers at the front of the line, and one leaned down to hug Reese, leading Wade to suspect that she'd been here more times that she'd let on.

He could hear snippets of their conversation, something to do with vodka and bottle service.

She looked back at Wade and mouthed, "Do you want to go in?"

He shrugged. This was her world, and he wanted to experience it. She'd been in his for the last several weeks, and he wanted to see just how different that had been for her.

She sure hadn't had linen tablecloths and fifteen forks at his grandmother's place. Hell, they'd had a few meals that hadn't required utensils at all. "Sure."

"Gawwdd, I need another drink sooo bad." Red Dress giggled and wrapped her arm around his waist. "Don't worry, Reese will get us in. Brock's probably already inside and has a table. He always gets bottle service and never stands in line." She spoke loudly into his ear to be heard above the noise of the music.

Brock? What the hell?

These must not be close friends of Reese's if they still thought she was with Brock. And as much as he wanted to experience her world, he did not need another run-in with Brock.

"Reese." He called her name, but the crowd was too loud, and she was handing the bouncer her credit card.

What? His manhood had taken enough of a blow when her dad had paid for dinner, but now Reese was paying their cover for this club.

He pushed forward to stop her, but was distracted as the blonde's hand slid from his waist down to grab ahold of his butt.

"Whoa there." He grabbed her hand and pushed it away. What the hell was going on?

"Oh goody!" she squealed and pressed forward as they followed Reese and Ms. Snotty up the stairs into the crowded club.

Not having much of a choice, he was swept up the stairs and pushed through the throng of people. They passed the dance floor, and the deep beat of the bass pounded in his chest as hordes of couples danced and writhed to the music.

They were herded into a round booth, and a waitress appeared, carrying a bottle of vodka in a bucket of ice and a tray of shot glasses.

Reese pulled him down onto the seat next to her and offered him an apologetic look.

Ms. Snotty leaned across him to speak loudly to the blonde. "Reese and Brock broke up. This is her date you've been molesting."

Red Dress giggled again and wrinkled her small nose up at him. "Oops, my bad. Lucky girl." She winked at Reese and pointed to the glasses. "Pour me a drink, honey. Let's get this party started."

What kind of crazy world did Reese live in? These girls were nuts.

Reese tipped her mouth up to speak loudly into his ear

as she pointed to Ms. Snotty and Red Dress. "This is Julie and Lisa."

She yelled his name to the two women. "This is my date, Wade. He's from Cotton Creek. It's a small town up in the mountains."

Julie was not impressed, giving him a slight nod then turning her attention back to the throng of people in the club. Probably looking for someone more interesting than him.

Lisa threw back another shot and leaned into his arm. "Nice to meet you, Cade. Pour me another one and then let's dance."

He poured another shot for her. "You all go ahead. I'll stay here and keep an eye on the table."

She giggled and downed the drink. "You don't have to. You really aren't from around here." She pointed at the bottle of vodka. "That's what bottle service is, silly. Reese got us that lovely two hundred and fifty dollar bottle of Grey Goose vodka, and it lets us sit here as long as we want."

Two hundred and fifty dollars? For one bottle of vodka. Ridiculous.

Before he had time to question Reese, Lisa was on her feet and pulling them out to the dance floor.

He was terrible at this kind of dancing, but the music was loud and the people were packed in so tight, all he'd have to do is sway a little and he should be fine.

Reese slid in next to him on the dance floor and slipped her arms around his neck. She put her mouth next to his ear and shouted, "Are you all right? I know this isn't what you were expecting."

He pulled her against him and tried to suppress his frown. "I'm fine. I just wish you wouldn't have wasted your money on getting us in here."

She rolled her eyes. "I know. I succumbed to peer pressure. What else is new?"

Her peers were now dancing with them, or at least that's what he thought they were doing.

It didn't seem much like dancing to him, more like grinding themselves against him and Reese.

The music was loud, and he could feel it beating through him. The room smelled like booze, cigarette smoke, expensive cologne and an underlying scent of weed.

The dim lighting added to the intoxicating blend of skin and movement as the three women danced around him. He was used to leading one woman around a dance floor and this just made him feel strange and uncomfortable at the same time.

The song changed, and Reese grabbed his hand and pulled him back to the table.

The two girls followed, and Lisa drunkenly slid into the seat next to him. Her face had the slack look of too much to drink and mascara smudged under her eyes.

She reached for the bottle and knocked over the bucket, the icy water pouring into Reese's lap.

Reese gasped as the cold water soaked into her lap.

Wade grabbed for the bucket before it could knock over the other drinks.

Lisa leaned against him. "I really don't feel so good."

She grabbed for the empty ice bucket, bent forward, and to Wade's horror, vomited into it.

Setting the bucket on the floor, she groaned and laid her head on Wade's lap.

"I think we need to get your friend a cab," Wade yelled to Reese and Julie. Reese had a horrified look on her face, but Julie wore the same look of passive indifference.

"Good luck with that," Julie said, nodding at her friend. "She's passed out. I told her not to drink so much."

Wade scooped the girl into his arms, and she laid her head against his shoulders, mumbling something about wanting to dance, but the room wouldn't stop spinning.

Reese grabbed her purse, and she and Julie followed in his wake as he carried the semi-conscious girl to the sidewalk in front of the club.

Reese hailed a cab. Wade deposited the girl into the backseat then handed the driver a twenty.

Julie offered Reese another air kiss before climbing into the cab with her friend. "See you around. Tell Brock I said hello when you see him next."

Wow. Really?

Wade narrowed his eyes at the little brat, wondering if perhaps she was in drag, because she had some balls.

Reese set a hand on his arm. "I'm so sorry about that. This night isn't turning out anything like I planned. Do you still want to try to go to that pub?"

He looked down at her soaked dress. "No. You can't go anywhere like that, and I think I've had about all the excitement I can stand for one evening." He ran a hand through his hair and blew out a sigh. He wanted to see the humor in the situation, share a good laugh about it with Reese.

But she wasn't laughing, and he wasn't feeling very amused. "Why don't we head back and get you into some dry clothes. Which way to your car?"

Reese held up a hand to hail another cab. "It's easier to just take a cab from here. I'll send one of the valets at my apartment building to pick up my car later."

Must be nice to be able to send someone to fetch your car. Like you'd send a dog after a bone.

Reese's life was so different from his. And she seemed different here.

She easily doled out instructions to staff members as if used to a life of privilege, but she didn't have the same confidence in herself that she'd had up in the mountains the last two weeks with him.

He hadn't heard her apologize in the whole two weeks as many times as she had tonight. And she seemed less decisive, as if waiting for him to tell her what to do.

Chalking it up to nerves, he slid into the cab with her as she gave the driver her address.

Nothing about this date had gone as he'd thought it would.

He sure hadn't expected to see her dad at the restaurant or have a drunk girl pass out on his lap. The only woman he'd hoped to carry was Reese on their way to bed, but that hadn't been the case, either.

Everything about tonight reminded him of the differences in their worlds and how separate their lives were from each other's. Reese seemed like a meek shell of the girl he'd spent the last few weeks with, and his manhood had taken several blows tonight.

She lived in a circle of wealth and privilege where money was thrown around easily and without thought. Or used to distinguish power or authority over others.

And he'd had no power over anything tonight. The only thing he'd even been allowed to pay for was the cab ride of her drunken friend.

Chapter Eleven

Reese unlocked the door to her apartment and dropped her keys back in her purse. She set her bag on the table inside the door and let out a heavy sigh. "I know this date probably didn't turn out like you thought it would. I'm really sorry."

"Quit apologizing." Wade's gruff tone matched the scowl on his face, and he dropped onto the sofa. He ran his hand through his hair and rubbed the back of his head. "It's not your fault."

She loved the way his bangs fell across his forehead, a forehead that was now creased with tension. She wanted to brush her fingers through his hair and caress his cheek.

Anything to wipe that disappointed frown from his face.

His scowl reminded her of when they'd first met, and she wasn't happy to see the expression return.

"I'm going to get out of this dress." She hoped he'd pick up on her subtle hint and offer to help, but he barely acknowledged her as he nodded. He seemed preoccupied and lost in thought.

She walked toward her bedroom. "Can you listen for the

door? The valet should be up any minute. My car keys are in my purse if you can just hand them to him."

Wade grunted in response and pushed off the sofa, not even turning her way.

Nothing about this night had gone like she'd planned.

Maybe because this wasn't the night she'd planned at all.

She pushed her bedroom door shut and tugged her sodden dress over her head. She'd had such hopes for tonight, hopes for Wade to see her again and remember how much fun they'd had together.

So far, nothing about tonight had been fun.

She couldn't believe Lisa had puked right in front of Wade. Why had she let Julie even talk her into going into the club?

And she'd wasted close to three hundred dollars on getting bottle service. She was still succumbing to peer pressure, yielding to someone else's needs.

Why?

She'd been doing so great since she'd been back from Cotton Creek. She'd even told her dad *no* on two separate occasions.

So why did she flounder tonight when it really mattered? Why didn't she just tell Wade that she'd made other plans for them?

Was she trying to impress him? If so, that plan had completely backfired.

Time for plan B.

Reaching for the little bag on her dresser, she pulled out the fun purchase she'd found online earlier that week.

She ran her fingers across the silken material of the satin and lace teddy and grinned at the green and brown camouflage pattern.

If her breasts peeking out of camo lingerie didn't make him smile, they really were in trouble.

She stepped into the teddy, luxuriating in the feel of the satin against her skin. Wade had shown her that she could be sexy and fun in the bedroom, and she felt as if she'd come alive the last few weeks.

He'd made her feel an entirely new range of emotions.

Okay, so tonight's date had been a bust, but she'd seen Wade in a new situation, completely out of his element, and he had still impressed her. He'd handled meeting her dad with confidence, and he'd even taken the fiasco of the club in stride.

Her friend had gotten drunk and sick, and he didn't even bat an eye. Just got down to business and took care of the situation. Her heart had melted a little when he'd picked Lisa up and carried her out of the club.

He may have been out of his comfort zone, but he'd tried to make the best of it. That's because Wade was one of the good guys. One of the ones you hear rumors about.

People are always saying there are good guys out there. And now she was sure she'd found one. She could actually see a future with Wade.

She knew one thing. She sure didn't want to see her future without him. There was still the little issue of them living two hours away from each other.

But she was working on that.

Pulling on a black lace robe, she cinched the belt around her waist and stepped back into the living room.

Wade stood by the front door. He had the soccer tickets in his hand and a puzzled expression on his face.

He looked up at her in confusion. "Did you buy these tickets for tonight?"

She nodded.

"Then why didn't we use them? It says here they cost sixty dollars apiece, and a soccer game sounds like a heck of a lot more fun than the night we just had."

She shrugged. "I know. I had a whole other evening

planned. I thought we would go to this Irish pub for fish and chips, then I would take you to the soccer game."

He arched an eyebrow at her. "You weren't really running late when I got here, were you? You were already dressed for our date?"

"Yeah. Sort of." She couldn't quite meet his eye.

"Why didn't you tell me?"

"You showed up here dressed in a suit, and you told me once that you only had one suit and it was reserved for funerals. So I knew you'd put in a lot of effort to dress up for me." She sighed. "I didn't want to disappoint you."

"Disappoint me? Hell, you would have made my night if you'd have told me to go grab my jeans out of the truck." He shook his head. "Why didn't you just talk to me?" Frustration and hurt lingered in his eyes.

Not used to seeing him this way, all she wanted to do was go to him and put her arms around him. She should have owned the date and told him about the tickets when he first got there. They might have even laughed about it.

She'd messed everything up.

Before she could take a step toward him, the doorbell rang.

Wade shook his head at her, then turned to open the door. A parking valet stood in the hallway. He held out his hand, and Wade passed him the keys.

"There're singles in my purse if you want to hand him a tip," she said.

His shoulders tightened, and his eyes narrowed in anger as he turned to her. "I can handle the tip." He reached for his wallet and passed the valet a five dollar bill.

"Thank you. We'll have your car back in the next hour, Ms. Hudson. Have a good evening." The valet turned to the elevator, and Wade shut the door.

Waves of anger emanated off Wade's skin like

thunderclouds before a storm. His eyes narrowed. "Do you think I'm so broke that I can't give the man a tip?"

She took a step back, unused to the anger in his voice. "No, of course not. I just didn't want you to have to use your money to get my car."

"How about tonight at dinner? Or getting us into the club? Do you realize you, or your father, didn't let me pay for a single thing tonight? Like I was a poor country hick that couldn't afford to cover your meal."

"Wade, stop it. I never think of you like that."

"Don't you?" He gestured his arms around her apartment. "How could you not? Look at this place. How could you ever be happy with anything I have to offer after you've been used to this all your life?"

He didn't give her a chance to answer. "Look, I'm just gonna go. There's no point in wasting our time anymore with something that has no future. Good-bye, Reese."

A look of pain crossed his face, then he turned and walked out the front door.

The soft click of the latch was deafening in the quiet room.

Reese stood frozen, unable to breathe. She felt like a giant vise was squeezing her chest.

What the hell had just happened?

What did he mean by wasting their time?

Indignation rose inside of her, releasing her from the frozen state. She charged forward, throwing the door open just in time to see the elevator doors slide shut.

Racing for the stairwell, she ran down the four flights of stairs, determined to catch him. Pushing through the door on the main level, she caught sight of him just as he stepped through the front doors and out on the street.

Gasping for breath, she rushed through the lobby and followed him out onto the street. The rough gravel bit at her bare feet, and she stopped and yelled at him. "Hey. Where the hell do you think you're going?"

He stopped in his tracks. He slowly turned around and his jaw dropped.

She was sure she must have looked a sight in her bare feet and tiny silk robe. A couple giggled as they passed by.

"What are you doing?" Wade took three strides back and stood in front of her, looking down at her in disbelief. He ripped his suit jacket off and wrapped it around her shoulders.

Taking a moment, she tried to slow her breathing. Between the stairs and her anger at him, her heart was pounding hard against her chest.

But this was no time to back down.

Planting her fists on her hips and jutting out her jaw, she stood her ground. "What do you mean there's no point in wasting our time? Do you consider the past few weeks with me a waste of your time?"

"What? No, of course not. These last few weeks with you have been amazing." Frustration creased his forehead. "But tonight showed me that I can't be what you need. I could never give you the things that you're used to."

"Who asked you to give me anything?"

A low roll of thunder sounded in the sky. Fat raindrops hit the sidewalk between them, but neither seemed to care.

He held her gaze but said nothing.

It almost hurt to breathe. But not as much as it would hurt if he walked out of her life.

The sidewalk darkened as the rain fell harder. A small puddle formed around her right foot.

She wanted to take control. To make her own decisions.

But Wade had to make his own decisions, too.

She took a deep breath. "Look, I think we have something here, and I'm not willing to just throw it away. If you don't want me, that's one thing. And that's fine. I get that. But don't run away."

His eyes widened, then a steely look crossed his face.

He took a step closer, and Reese backed up into the brick wall of her apartment building. Her gaze locked with his, and she couldn't tear her eyes away.

Gripping her arms, he pressed his body against her. "Wanting you has never been the problem." He dipped his head, his lips dangerously close to hers. His voice was gruff with need. "I've wanted you with everything in me from the first day I laid eyes on you."

This was it. This was her chance to make her own decision, decide her own fate.

He wasn't telling her what to do.

She could make up her own mind. If this was what she wanted or not.

And Wade Baker was definitely what she wanted.

And she wanted him now.

She narrowed her eyes and slid her arms around his waist. His breath caught as she gripped his shirt in her fists and pulled him tighter against her.

Gathering her courage, she swallowed, then spoke, her words clear and strong. "Then take me."

He hesitated, only a moment, then crushed his lips against hers.

One of his hands gripped the back of her head, and the other cupped her cheek as he feasted on her mouth, drawing her in as if she were his carnal delight.

His kisses trailed from her lips, across her cheek, down her throat. His suit jacket fell to the ground as his hands slipped inside of her robe, baring her shoulders.

The rain beat down on her skin, soaking the silk fabric of the robe.

Droplets of rain ran down her chest, but his lips were warm, leaving a line of heat everywhere they touched.

Despite the cool rain, her body burned with heat, and she

wouldn't have been surprised to see steam rising off her skin.

His hand slipped around her waist, pulling her hips against his and leaving no doubt that the want he spoke of was real.

His lips found hers again, and she moaned against his mouth.

The brick wall dug into her back, but she didn't care. People walked by them on the sidewalk, but she didn't care about that, either.

Nothing mattered except this moment with this man. Let them look.

As long as he didn't stop kissing her. Didn't stop touching her.

A shiver ran through her, and he pulled back, his breath ragged as he looked down at her. He shook his head as if coming to his senses.

No. Don't come to your senses. Stay in this crazy moment with me. Don't go.

"Aw hell, what am I doing?"

She gripped his waist. "You are doing everything exactly right."

"You must be freezing." He grabbed his jacket off the ground then dipped down and slid his arm behind her knees. Lifting her off her feet, he cradled her against his chest. "Let's get you inside."

She curled against his chest, letting him carry her into the lobby of her apartment building and into the elevator.

He pushed the button for her floor, and the doors slid shut.

He looked down at her. Her robe had fallen open and he took in the green shaded lingerie. A slow smile spread across his face. "What in the world are you wearing?"

"It's a camouflage teddy."

The silk fabric was wet and clung to her breasts, the hardened tips of her nipples partially visible through the black lace edging.

Wade's eyes roamed over her body, and she swore she could feel the heat in his gaze. "Well, it's not camouflaging much."

The bell chimed, and the elevator doors opened on the second floor.

A little old lady carrying a handbag the size of Texas stepped on and nodded at Reese and Wade. A curly-haired white poodle poked his head out of the corner of the purse.

Holding back a giggle, Reese tried to maintain her composure. "Good evening, Mrs. Windish. How was your bridge night?"

The older woman huffed. "Gladys from the third floor cheated on the second hand, and the Chex mix was stale. I swear Velma just freezes it every week and then thaws it again for bridge night." She gave Wade a once-over with her eyes while the poodle sniffed his elbow. "Who's this strapping young man?"

The warmth of a blush crept up Reese's cheeks. "This is Wade."

"I'm her boyfriend." Wade nodded his head and offered Mrs. Windish one of his charming smiles.

She didn't know about Mrs. Windish, but Reese was pretty sure that smile just melted her panties right off.

He'd just called himself her boyfriend.

She couldn't hold back the grin that now took over her face. "Wade, this is Mrs. Elaine Windish. She lives down the hall from me."

"Pleased to meet you, ma'am."

The white-haired woman raised an eyebrow at Reese's attire as the bell chimed for their floor. "My husband was quite an outdoorsman. I wonder if I had worn something similar to that, if he'd have 'tracked' me down more often in the bedroom."

The elevator doors slid open on her floor. She waved and offered Wade a saucy wink. "Happy hunting, Mr. Boyfriend."

Reese laughed. A loud hearty laugh as he carried her to her front door.

She reached down and turned the knob, thankful that she hadn't bothered to lock the front door in her haste to follow Wade.

He stepped into the room, pushed the door shut with his hip, toed his shoes off, then purposely strode sock-footed through her bedroom and into the master bathroom.

Pulling open the glass door, he set her down inside the large walk-in shower and turned on the warm water.

Dropping his jacket, he stripped off his suit pants and tossed them on the floor.

He reached for his tie, but she stopped him, setting her hands on top of his. "Let me."

She loosened the knot and slowly pulled the tie from around his neck.

Steam filled the bathroom as she flicked each button of his dress shirt open, laying a kiss against his skin beneath each opened button.

Releasing the last one, she slid her arms inside the shirt, lightly trailing her fingernails along his stomach and up his chest. She slid the shirt off his shoulders, leaning forward to lay a kiss against the taut muscles of his chest.

His breath caught, and she pressed herself against the male hardness straining against his black boxer briefs.

He reached for the belt of her robe, freeing the cinched knot and letting the silky fabric fall open. She straightened her arms and let the robe drop to the shower floor.

Standing in front of him, clad only in the tiny satin and lace teddy, she knew this was exactly where she wanted to be. And he was the man she wanted to be with. He didn't try to control her. He let her make her own decisions.

And right now, she was deciding that camouflage was the last thing she needed. Reaching for the spaghetti straps, she slid them from her shoulders and let the silky fabric fall.

He said nothing, just watched as she drew the teddy lower, sliding it over her hips and letting it fall in a puddle at her feet.

She looked up into his eyes. "I don't want to camouflage what I feel for you. I'm not hiding it. I like you, Wade Baker. I like you a lot, and I want you in my life."

"I like you, too." He grinned. "You're not making this much of a hunt."

She smiled back, but her words were serious. "I'm not making you hunt for me. I'm not disguising myself. I'm standing right in front of you. The question is, are you going to catch me?"

"Damn right I am." He bent and slipped his arms around her waist, lifting her and pressing her back against the shower wall.

The air was steamy, and she wrapped her legs around his waist, drawing him tighter to her.

His lips crushed hers, the heat of his desire rivaling the steamy warmth of the shower.

She'd never done this before in the shower, and the wildness of the act thrilled her. Feeling vulnerable to Wade's strength at holding her against the wall, she gripped his arms and tipped her head back in rapture.

Water cascaded down her chest as he nipped and kissed her throat.

Arching her back, she moaned as his tongue circled her swollen nipple before sucking it into his mouth.

Every place that Wade touched her sent pleasure wrenching through her body.

Trying to catch her breath, her quick pants of anticipation seemed to fuel his desire, evident by his rock-hard maleness pressing against her tender skin.

She trembled in his arms as her body craved his.

His voice was husky as he spoke against her ear. "I want you, Reese. I need to be inside you."

"Yes," was all she could say. And she said it more than once.

"Hold on." He set her down and eased from the shower, dripping water across the floor as he peeled his briefs off, then grabbed his pants and dug out his wallet. Pulling out a condom, he quickly unwrapped it and fit it on before stepping back into the shower.

Sliding his muscular arms around her back, he lifted her, pressing her into the wall as his hands cupped her butt. The steam rose from the shower, but it was nothing compared to the heat coming off Wade's body.

Everything about this man was magnificent, and she wanted him. All of him.

Raking her hands along his back, she cried out as he entered her.

The tiled shower wall was cold and hard against her back, but she didn't care. She didn't care about anything except this man and the steady rhythm of his hips crashing into hers.

The hot water beat against her skin as Wade's fingers clenched her ass, drawing her tighter against him with each thrust.

She filled her hands with his wet hair, clutching his head and crying out from the pure pleasure.

His gruff sounds matched hers, and she clung to him as he took her to the edge. Then she was falling over, bliss filling her with each tremor of abandon.

He met her stroke for stroke, and she reveled in his release.

She melted into him, letting his body claim hers. His breath came hard as she freed her legs from his waist. Her legs trembled as she tried to stand, and she was glad he still had an arm around her waist.

He grinned down at her. "Wow. You're quite a catch."

She laughed, looking up at him, trying to express her unspoken promise that she really was his captive.

He had captured not just her body, but her heart and soul. "Now that you've caught me, you know that means I'm yours."

His eyes were tender as he smiled down at her. "Babe, I've been yours since the night I took you fishing, and you pulled me out of the boat. You ended up hooking me that night. And as much as I've pulled on the line, I'm done fighting it, I belong to you now. I just hope you're not planning to catch and release me."

Her heart melted. He said just the words she needed to hear.

A huge grin spread across her face. "Oh, I do have plans for you. I'm not letting you go, but I might try for a few more releases."

He laughed and turned off the water in the shower. Grabbing a towel, he wrapped it around her wet body and drew her to him. "I do love a woman who can create a good fishing sex metaphor."

Did he just say he loved her?

He'd pulled back and grabbed another towel. His eyes were covered as he toweled off his hair so she couldn't read if he really meant that or if it was just a slip of the tongue.

Wade dropped the towel and grabbed her, lifting her up and carrying her into the bedroom.

His grin was broad, and she let his comment go as he asked, "What kind of bait do I need to get you into that bed?"

"You're already 'luring' me in with all this romantic fish talk." She laughed as he set her on the bed and nuzzled her neck.

"Good, my plan is working."

He climbed into bed with her, and she wrapped her arms around his neck. He'd just said he was hers, and she wasn't letting him off the line.

Chapter Twelve

Wade padded barefoot into the kitchen. The morning sun shone through the window above the sink, and he caught himself humming a song he'd heard on the radio.

Last night with Reese had been amazing.

He felt good. Like they really did have a future. Last night had been rough, but they'd made it through. They might actually have a chance at something real here.

The cabinet above the coffeemaker held filters and ground beans, and he started a pot of coffee brewing and searched for a cup.

Images of Reese naked filled his head as he watched the dark liquid drip into the carafe. Reese in the shower, soapy water sliding off her body. Reese on the bed, her blond hair spread out across the pillows.

After filling his cup, he brought it to his lips and took a sip. The hot liquid burned his lip, and he sloshed brown coffee down the front of his shirt. *Great.*

He'd hung his pants and dress shirt over the shower the night before so they were dry, but totally wrinkled as he put them on this morning. The coffee stain just added to his general look of dishevelment.

He needed to get out to his truck and get his duffle bag. He'd brought a clean change of clothes and his cowboy boots. He ran his hand along his whisker-stubbled chin. A shave wouldn't hurt, either.

Reese's phone buzzed on the kitchen counter, and he looked down at the screen. A text popped up with his name in the message, and he couldn't help himself.

Tilting his head, he could view the message from "Dad" reading:

> *Regarding Wade—You've made your point. Now can you please get back to work? And can you come get your dog this morning? He threw up in my shoe.*

She'd made her point?
What the hell did that mean?

Was dating him just a way to prove something to her dad? Was he some kind of lower class jab to get under her dad's skin?

At least he wasn't the only one who'd been puked on last night.

He grinned at the thought of Bagel hurling into one of Robert Hudson's best loafers. Hell, he didn't even own a pair of loafers. And the dress shoes he'd worn last night had given him a blister on his heel.

He felt like he'd been playing at some kind of dress-up game where he'd worn a costume just to impress a girl.

Thoughts of filling his hands with Reese's luscious curves filled his mind. Dang, she was quite a girl.

But was she worth all of this? Of his acting like someone he wasn't? Of fights on the street in the rain? Of her chasing him down in her undies?

Where the hell did she even find camo underwear?

He needed to get his boots back on. And he needed to get some air. Too many thoughts were crowding his head, and he didn't like the direction of any of them.

Well, except the camo nightie ones, those were some pretty good thoughts.

Grabbing a Post-it off the counter, he scribbled a note telling Reese he was going for a walk.

Stuffing his bare feet into his dress shoes, he grabbed his keys and quietly slipped out the door.

· · ·

Reese rolled over in the bed and stretched like a cat.

Her body felt stiff, and she grinned at the thought of what had caused the stiffness. Wade.

She reached for him, but the other side of the bed was empty.

A momentary flash of panic filled her that he'd left again, but the smell of coffee filled the air. He must be in the kitchen.

Maybe she could persuade him to have breakfast in bed, and by breakfast, she meant coffee with a side of her. All sides.

She reached for her robe then changed her mind. Grinning like a fool, she threw back her shoulders and paraded naked into the living room.

But the room was empty. And so was the kitchen.

She spied Wade's note on the counter and read it as she poured herself a cup of coffee. The coffee was still warm so he couldn't have left too long ago.

Her phone buzzed, making a clicking sound as it bounced against the granite countertops.

Crud. Four messages from her dad.

And all about Bagel.

Her dad was normally great with the little dog. She sometimes thought he preferred the dog's company over hers. Why was he so adamant about her getting the dog this morning?

Her dad's apartment was three blocks from hers. She could be there and back within ten minutes. She sighed, abandoning her plans for a leisurely morning in bed.

Oh well. They could always have lunch in bed. And an afternoon snack.

She quickly brushed her hair and teeth, then threw on yoga pants, a sweatshirt and some flip-flops. A bra would have been a good idea since she was going to see her dad, but she planned to be in and out, grab the dog and get back here as quickly as possible.

And the fewer clothes she had between her and Wade today, the better.

She wrote "Went to grab Bagel from my dad's. Back in ten minutes—be naked," on the bottom of Wade's note then smiled in anticipation as she headed out the door.

• • •

Wade knocked on the door, hoping Reese was up.

He juggled the tray of coffees and bag of donuts he'd picked up on his walk. In the past few weeks he'd turned her into a fan of maple icing, and the bag contained two large cinnamon rolls slathered in the stuff.

He wasn't sure if she'd feel like hot coffee or iced this morning, so he got her both. His backpack lay heavy against his shoulder as he reached up to knock again.

The door swung open, and he almost dropped the bag of rolls.

What the hell?

"Hello, Wayne." Brock stood in the open doorway of Reese's apartment, a smug grin on his face.

"It's Wade," he said, as he pushed past him into the living

room.

The cloying scent of flowers overpowered the room from the dozens of vases of red roses scattered around the room. He crossed to the kitchen and set the coffee and donuts on the counter. "Think you might have got a little carried away with the flowers?"

Brock offered him a contemptuous smile. "Reese loves red roses."

No, she doesn't, you ass.

She loves purple asters and the bright orange Indian paintbrush flowers that grew next to the path on the way up to Cotton Creek Falls. She loved the yellow sweet clover that grew like crazy all over his grandmother's property and that she filled Mason jars with to keep on the table beside her bed.

Brock's obvious confidence in himself and in being in Reese's apartment infuriated Wade.

He looked around the room, spying his note crumpled and on the floor by the refrigerator. "Where is Reese?"

"She went out to grab a bottle of champagne."

Wade wanted to slap the condescending sneer from Brock's face. "Isn't it a little early in the day for champagne?"

"We're celebrating. I've officially asked Reese to marry me." He pulled a ring box from his pocket and popped it open. A huge diamond sparkled against the red velvet interior of the box. "And she's accepted."

"That's bullshit."

Seeing that ring sent a river of dread churning through his gut. A small part of his brain asked why she wasn't wearing the ring, but the bigger part of his ego took over and crushed any kind of logic his brain was trying to find.

That was one hell of a huge rock. Who was going to say no to that?

"Is it?" Brock straightened his cuffs in an obvious gesture of arrogance. "Look, Wayne, everyone knows the score here.

Everyone, except you, it seems. Even Reese's father is on board with our engagement. He told me he'd met you last night when I was over at his apartment this morning asking for his daughter's hand in marriage."

Was that true? Maybe Reese was with her father now.

Why the hell wasn't she here, telling him this herself?

He glanced at Brock, studied him.

The man was beyond handsome. He looked as if he'd stepped out of a magazine, his designer suit crease free, gold cuff links winking from his sleeves. His dark hair was perfect and his teeth sparkling white as he grinned disdainfully at Wade.

One more punch to his fragile ego, he cursed himself for still wearing the rumpled suit. The coffee stain down the front of his white shirt added to his feeling of looking like a homeless guy off the street. And he was sure his hair stood up in its typical early morning bed-head style.

He must look like a total loser to this guy.

Hell, he *was* a loser compared to this guy.

The flames of his insecurities sparked to life, and his inadequacies overtook him. He scanned Reese's apartment. He would never be able to keep her in the style she was used to.

And he sure as hell would never be able to afford to give her a diamond anywhere close to that size.

He didn't even own a house. He lived on his grandmother's property in the caretaker's cottage.

Who was he kidding? Reese would never be happy with him. Painful memories of Tawnya's rejection filled his head, and his already fragile ego deflated like a saggy over-stretched balloon. Tawnya had been a middle-class girl trying to live beyond her means, and he didn't even make enough money to keep *her* happy.

Reese was used to living in wealth and luxury. She might

be happy with him for a while, but then the glow would wear off, and she would miss this lavish life. She would have to.

You made your point. Her dad's text message crossed his mind.

Was this all some way for her to get attention from her dad?

Robert Hudson had one little girl, and he was clearly an overprotective father. How would he ever accept Wade in her life, when the bar had been set so high by Brock-freaking-fancy-pants financial advisor?

He didn't need this. This constant barrage of pain to his heart. The push and pull of trying to make a relationship with Reese work. The drama.

Suddenly Wade felt bone tired. Fatigued to his very core. He was tired of competing in this contest that he didn't have a chance in hell of winning.

It was easier to be alone.

And it hurt a hell of a lot less.

And where was Reese? Why had she crumpled up his note?

Her absence made things pretty clear to Wade.

She obviously wanted to be with Brock and didn't have the balls to face him. Why else would she leave the apartment and not wait to tell him herself that she wanted to break it off?

Maybe the text from her dad had gotten to her and made her see what a mistake she was making.

He looked at Brock, and bile rose in his throat from the look of scorn and pity that he saw in the other man's eyes.

Clutching the strap of his backpack so hard his knuckles turned white, he struggled to hold back from punching this pompous ass in the throat.

"You know what? You can have her. I already got what I needed." He brushed by Brock, nudging him with his shoulder as he passed, feeling a slight sense of satisfaction as he saw Brock's mask of contempt slip just for a second.

He was done with this girl, done with this town.

He pushed open the door of the apartment building and strode down the sidewalk toward his truck.

His heart beat hard against his chest, anger and hurt swirling through his gut.

Let her go back to the arrogant S-O-B. They deserved each other.

He tried to ignore the next question. *What do I deserve?*

Chapter Thirteen

"Seriously, Dad. Wade is a great guy. He really cares about me." Reese cuddled the fat pug against her chest. She'd spent too long at her dad's apartment already.

Wade was probably already back at her place.

And if he'd followed her instructions on the note, and was naked, she didn't want to waste any more time getting back to him.

Her dad sighed. "I'm sure he is, honey. I was glad to finally get to meet him, and I told you that you made your point. He did seem like a decent enough guy."

She arched an eyebrow at him.

"All right. He seemed like a nice guy. And I could tell he was really trying." Robert dragged a tanned hand through his thick dark hair. "But I want my little girl to have more than just a nice guy. I want you to have everything."

Her heart softened a little at her dad's tone. Just like it always did. But she didn't want this to be just like every other time. She was done bending to her dad's will. She wanted to take control, and the only way to do that was to stand up to her dad.

She lifted her chin. "Sometimes having a nice, cute guy *is* everything." She hefted the dog against her chest. "And that nice cute guy is waiting for me back at my apartment so I've got to go, Dad."

A shocked look passed over Robert's face. "Wait. Did you say Wade's at your apartment now? He spent the night?"

Reese shook her head. "Dad, I'm a grown woman. I don't need to ask your permission to have a sleepover."

"No, of course not. It's not that." A questioning look crossed his face. "Are you really serious about this Wade guy?"

She took a step closer to her dad and laid a hand gently on his arm. "Dad, that's what I've been trying to tell you. Not only am I serious about him, I'm in love with him."

"Oh, shit."

She froze. She knew the sound of that two-word phrase, and it was never good.

She squeezed her dad's arm, and Bagel leaned in and tried to lick his face. "Oh shit, what? Dad?"

He cleared his throat. "Brock was over here this morning, and he asked me for your hand in marriage."

Her heart slammed against her chest, and her eyes blinked. Once. Twice. "And what did you tell him?"

Her father swallowed, his eyes looking anywhere but at her. She'd never seen him nervous like this before. "Well, I guess I gave him my blessing."

"You guess?"

"Okay. Yes. I gave him my blessing. And I might have sent him over to your apartment to surprise you."

"What?" She stared at him in shocked disbelief. "Dad, you didn't."

Brock was on his way to her apartment now? And Wade was there waiting for her. Oh my Lord.

And if he had followed her instructions, he was waiting naked.

She turned and raced for the door.

It couldn't have taken her more than five minutes to reach her apartment door.

Her breath came hard and fast as she inserted her key and opened the door. The smell of roses overpowered her as she stepped into the room, and Bagel let out a yip.

Her heart sank at the sight of the man standing at her kitchen counter, a takeout coffee in his hand and a smug look on his face.

"Brock. What are you doing here? And where's Wade?"

"Hello, Reese. I thought you'd be a little more excited to see me. It's been weeks." He gestured around the room. "Aren't you going to thank me for the flowers?"

Was he serious? "No, you can take your flowers and shove them."

She'd never spoken to him that way, and he arched an eyebrow at her. "Now Reese, there's no need to be rude. Obviously your time slumming it has caused a slip in your manners."

Two maple-iced donuts lay on a white takeout bag on the counter. Had Wade bought the donuts knowing they were now her favorite?

Where was he?

Brock picked up a donut, and she wanted to smack it from his hands.

He took a bite and licked the caramel-colored frosting from his lips. "Old Wayne does have pretty good taste in donuts, though."

A surge of adrenaline coursed through her blood.

Drawing strength from it, she straightened her shoulders and spoke through gritted teeth. "His. Name. Is. Wade."

She marched toward him, gaining power with each step.

Reaching up, she knocked the rest of the donut from his hands, and it hit the floor.

Brock stared wide-eyed at her as if he couldn't believe she'd done that. She almost couldn't believe it herself.

The only sound in the room was Bagel's toenails as he raced across the floor to gobble up the fallen pastry.

Brock laughed.

But not the kind of laugh where you're both in on the joke. This was a mean laugh, full of malice and ridicule.

"Yes, I can see you've picked up more than a few bad habits from hanging out with your country bumpkin. We'll have to work on breaking you of those, but I'm sure we can get back to our regular routine during the engagement. We'll want to get the club booked now for the wedding as I'm sure it fills up fast."

Break her of those bad habits? Did he really just say that? Like she was an unruly dog that needed to be retrained. To obey.

Had this been how he had always seen her? As a pet that heeled to his commands?

Well, this was *not* how he was ever going to see her again.

She narrowed her eyes at him. "You know what, Brock? You're right. For once I agree with you. I do have some bad habits that I need to break. And listening to egotistical asses like yourself is the first one on my list."

She took a tiny bit of pleasure from the way his mouth dropped open. Using one of Miss Abigail's favorite sayings, she told him, "Close your mouth. You'll catch flies that way."

He closed his mouth. This seemed to be working. For once, he was actually complying with *her* demands.

She gestured to the flowers scattered around the room. "I do not want your roses. And I do not need your condescending attitude. There's no need to book the club because I do *not* want to marry you."

Her voice gained strength with each pronouncement. "As a matter of fact, I don't even want to look at you. I want you to tell me where Wade is, then get the hell out of my apartment. And don't come back."

He spit malice, and his eyes flashed anger as he stomped to the door. "You know you're making a huge mistake. Women who are a lot better than you would kill to be dating a man like me."

"Let 'em. You're free now." And so was she.

A weight the size of a boulder felt as if it were being lifted from her shoulders. She laughed at the pure freedom she felt the closer he got to the door.

"Don't expect to come crawling back to me once you come to your senses."

She shook her head, feeling lighter and calmer with each level of anger that he descended to. "There will be no crawling. And for the first time in my life, I *have* completely come to my senses. And all on my own."

He yanked open the front door then turned for one final parting shot. "For your information, your new boyfriend already took off. He said he was done with you, and I'm sure he and his rumpled suit are halfway back to Jellystone Park by now. He looked like a bum when he was here earlier. I almost handed him a twenty when he knocked on the door."

Oh no. Her sense of calm came crashing down as Brock slammed the door behind him.

He's gone?

Brock must have filled his head with a bunch of garbage. But why would he leave?

She grabbed for her phone and punched in his number. Chewing the corner of her thumbnail, she listened as it rang four colossally long rings then went to voicemail. Her heart twisted a little as she heard Wade's easy-going voice instructing her to leave a message.

She hung up and tried again. Come on, Wade. Pick up. Pick UP.

"Hello."

Limp with relief, she sank into the corner of the couch. "Wade, where are you? Brock said you left town."

"Yeah, Brock had a lot of things to say. I'm sure you two will be very happy."

"Wade, listen, it's not how it seems." If he would just give her a chance to explain.

"It appears that nothing is exactly what it seems with you. And I don't need this nonsense in my life anymore."

"What are you saying?"

"I'm saying that I'm done. I'm out." His voice hitched a little as if the words pained him. "Listen, I'm coming up to the tunnel, I've got to go. Bye, Reese." He hung up with a definitive click.

She stared at the phone in her hand, too stunned to move.

What the heck had just happened? She woke up this morning achy and sore from a night of amazing sex with a hot ranger, and now her heart was what ached as he told her they were through.

Well, guess what, buddy? She was done with people telling her what to do.

Grabbing her purse, she told Bagel to stay, then pulled the door shut behind her as she raced to get to her car.

Wade had said he was coming up to the tunnel so she knew exactly where he was on the road, and he was less than thirty minutes away.

She'd spent the last few weeks standing up for herself and taking control of her life, but now it felt as if the one thing that mattered the most was out of her control.

Chapter Fourteen

"Women. Who needs 'em?" Wade muttered as he threw the last of his camping gear in the back of his truck.

What he needed now was a few days away. Alone. Just him and the line full of fish he planned to catch.

He'd done it. He'd made a clean break. Told her they were through. So why did he feel like shit? Like a total heel for telling her he was out over the phone?

And what did she care?

Maybe he'd just made it easier on her to go off with Brock the Cock. Jerk.

Why did he feel so bad? And why did he feel like he might just be letting the best thing that had ever happened to him slip away?

How could she be the best thing when all she brought with her was drama and pain? And heartache.

And laughter. And joy. And great, amazing, mind-blowing sex.

He shook his head and slammed the tailgate of his truck closed.

It was over.

She'd made her choice. He didn't need to talk it to death. That's why he'd ignored the next twelve times she'd tried to call him.

And maybe because a small part of him knew if he answered, he'd take her back.

No. He was done.

He didn't need to drag it out any longer. No use beating a dead horse. It was easier to not answer the phone. Hell, maybe he'd leave the damn thing here for the next few days.

He didn't know what he'd say to her if he answered the phone anyway.

. . .

Reese screeched to a stop in front of Wade's truck. Thank goodness she'd caught him. She'd called up to the bed and breakfast and spoken to Wade's grandmother.

Miss Abigail had said Wade was stomping around, filling his truck with what looked like enough camping supplies for a month.

Reese had told her about the misunderstanding with Brock and that she wanted to at least have the chance to talk to Wade.

Ever the co-conspirator, Miss Abigail promised to do her best to keep Wade on the property until she could get there. Knowing Wade's grandmother, she'd concocted a distraction that could be anything from faking a heart attack to a stove-top fire.

Hopefully Reese would make it there before she had to resort to anything too crazy or that might involve burning the house down.

Wade's grandmother wasn't the only call she'd made on her way up the mountain. She'd also called her father.

After a quick explanation about kicking Brock out of her apartment and her impromptu trip into the mountains to find Wade, she asked him to go pick up Bagel from her apartment.

And before she lost her nerve, she'd also informed him that she was quitting her job.

"Just like that? Come on, Reese. You need to think about this." Her dad was using his *let's all just calm down* voice.

But it wasn't working. Not this time. "I have thought about it, Dad. This is not a decision that I'm making on a whim. I've wanted to quit this job for years, but just never had the guts to tell you."

Robert Hudson had cleared his throat. "Well, it seems like you're making quite a few gutsy decisions today."

She'd grinned into the phone. "Yes, I am. And it's about damn time. Don't forget to get Bagel. Bye, Dad."

She'd made one more call before pulling into the bed and breakfast.

A call that could change her life.

Change both of their lives.

The call had gone better than expected, but all of her bravado slipped away as she turned off the car and faced the angry man who stood by his truck.

She stepped from the car, suddenly self-conscious of her sweatshirt and yoga pants.

Running a hand through her hair, she wished she'd taken a few minutes to fix her hair or throw on a dab of mascara. Thank goodness she'd taken the time to brush her teeth before heading to her dad's.

He'd changed clothes, and her heart ached at how staggeringly good-looking he was. Trademark jeans, cowboy boots, and a faded blue T-shirt—just the way she liked him.

A memory of her wearing that same T-shirt and nothing else had her catching her breath. She could almost feel the soft cotton against her bare skin and Wade's hands skimming along under the hem of the shirt to caress her hip.

What would she do if he really didn't want her back?

How could she accept never kissing him again? Touching him? Laughing with him?

She just wouldn't accept it. She couldn't. It would break her heart.

She approached him slowly, gauging his reaction to her being here.

His reaction did not look good.

No happy greeting or welcoming embrace. Just the dark scowl reminiscent of the first time they'd met. She'd hoped she was done seeing that face.

Her voice was soft, tentative, as she gave him a little wave. "Hi."

He sighed and ran a hand across his whisker-stubbled chin. "What are you doing here? I told you we were through."

A shot of pain, like a physical punch to the stomach, ran through her, and she swallowed back the tears that threatened to fall. She would not cry.

She was the new and improved Reese. The one who took control and made decisions. And went after what she wanted. "I don't accept that."

He laughed. A harsh dry sound that was not amused at all. "Well, darlin', I hate to tell you, but you don't get a choice in the matter."

She stood her ground. Would not fumble.

Pushing back her shoulders, she took a step closer.

Now standing within inches of him, she could smell the light scent of detergent on his freshly washed shirt. She could see the fine blond hairs on his arms and the jagged white line of a small scar on his wrist.

All she wanted to do was reach out—touch him. Fall into his arms and laugh about how this had all been a mistake.

But Wade's expression held no amusement. His eyes held

only pain and disappointment.

Pain that she had put there. Whether it was intentional or not.

"Listen, I don't know what Brock told you, but I am *not* marrying him. The idea is preposterous. I kicked him out of the house and told him to take his flowers and his ring and shove them."

A small glimmer of surprise crossed his face, then was replaced again with the scowl. "That was a pretty big rock to just toss away. You sure you want to do that?"

"Of course I'm sure." His comment rankled something in her and sparked a sudden flare of anger. "You'd have known that if you'd waited to talk to me instead of running off."

His eyes widened. "You're seriously mad at *me* now?"

"Yeah, I guess so. I'm trying to make this work, Wade. I care about you. I just spent the last two hours chasing you up this damn mountain to tell you that. And I spent those two hours making some serious changes in my life. Changes that affect us."

"What kind of changes?"

"For starters, I called my dad and quit my job."

"You what? Why? And how does that affect *us*?"

"I quit the job that's made me miserable the last five years, and I accepted a job here. In Cotton Creek."

"Here?"

"Yep. I had an interview with Harry Langston, Miss Abigail's friend, before I left. He's been mentoring me with my writing, and he offered me a job at his newspaper. I told him I'd think about it, and I called him on my way up to tell him I'd accept the job. And I've spent the last few weeks working on how to get moved up here."

"Hold on there. You're moving up here?"

She couldn't tell if his voice sounded happy or horrified. Or both.

"Yes. I rented that big blue house on Main Street. It's only two blocks from the paper. Harry said I would be writing articles and helping with some of the clerical work, and if I had free time, I was welcome to work on my novel. Which, by the way, he's been helping me edit, and he said my story is quite good and holds a lot of promise."

"Well, didn't this all work out conveniently? And how will a job at a small-town paper support you? Or is your dad paying for this little experiment?"

All the air left her lungs, as if he had physically slapped her. "For your information, I have plenty of savings, and I can support myself. And none of this was *convenient*. Harry and I talked at the dance and he told me he'd take a look at my book and that I could try writing some articles for him. I stopped by the paper that week and got to talking to his main reporter who was close to having a baby and thinking of quitting her job. I got the idea then and for once in my life, went after something I wanted. I started doing research and submitting articles to him. I found a house to rent on my own and found a friend to sublet my place in the city. I've been working my ass off to make this happen. My dad has nothing to do with this—so screw you, Wade."

Her breath was coming hard as she spat out the words, talking too fast and too loud. "I did this because I want something different. I want to try something new. Something that I picked for myself. And because I want a life with you."

He ran a hand through his hair and let out a weary sigh. "That's just it, Reese. I *don't* want a life with you. This is too hard. Too much drama. I just want a simple life. And our lives are too different." He shook his head. "Plus, your dad will never accept me."

"Who cares?"

"You do. Or you will. Whether he's too protective or not, you're his only daughter, and you two have a bond. I don't want to be the one to stand in the way of that. And I know he'll probably let you try this little experiment, then he'll start pressuring you to leave me and go back to Denver, and you'll go."

She was stunned. Hadn't she just been telling him how she was breaking away from her dad's control? "You're wrong."

"Am I? This is a different world than you're used to. There's no theater or elegant restaurants for me to take you to. Your fancy little car is always gonna be covered in dust, and there's no shopping malls or department stores. You think you want this, but you'll eventually want back that wealth and luxury you're used to. You'll get tired of small-town life, and you'll get tired of me. I'm just saving us both the heartache by leaving you first."

"You're not saving me any heartache. You're breaking my heart right now. Please don't do this."

"I'm sorry, Reese." He climbed into the truck, his own eyes filled with the same pain she felt. "It's not worth it. It's over." He slammed the truck door, as if emphasizing the closing of their relationship.

Why was he doing this?

She knew he cared about her. He had to.

How could the last few weeks mean nothing to him? Maybe she hadn't really meant anything to him at all.

Maybe she'd just been a distraction, something to pass the time. She had to know.

She clung to the open window of the truck, desperate to hear the truth. "Wade, please, if you don't want me in your life, I guess I have to accept that. But I just need to know that these last few weeks meant something to you. That *I* meant something to you. Just tell me that I mattered. Give me one small sign that shows that you cared about me."

His voice broke as he quietly said, "I can't." He started the engine and threw the truck in reverse.

She lifted her hands from the window of the truck, her last connection to him broken.

Gravel flew as he put the truck in gear and sped down the driveway.

Chapter Fifteen

Reese couldn't believe it.

She drove down the mountain in stunned silence. What had just happened?

Last night, she'd had it all, with a cherry on top. A cherry in the form of a hot ranger filling her bed.

Now she had nothing.

She passed the sign for Cotton Creek Falls and rubbed a hand across her aching chest. As if on autopilot, she turned into the parking lot and parked in front of the new outhouse.

The outhouse that she and Wade had built.

She was tempted to burn it down again, just to bring them back together. But she couldn't do that. They'd built it together, and it meant something to her even if it didn't mean anything to him.

It was almost laughable. Wouldn't it have been fun to tell their friends that they'd met because she'd burned down his outhouse?

Memories of the last few weeks filled her head—the sound of Wade's electrical drill, the dry woodsy scent of sawdust, she and Wade in the bathtub at the inn, in front of the fire at the lake.

He'd taught her so much. How to fish, how to pound a nail, how to measure twice and cut once. He'd introduced her to maple-iced donuts and picnics in a boat and the best fried chicken she'd ever tasted.

He had made her feel. Feel like she had worth.

Feel sexy. Feel like a woman. Feel alive.

And she loved it.

She loved him.

She sighed as she got out of the car, a deep shuddering sigh. Her feet took her to the path, and she walked slowly up toward the falls.

The rushing water of the waterfall filled her vision as she rounded the corner to the outlook. How could he throw her away? Act like this never happened?

All she'd wanted was one hint, one clue, anything to show that he had cared about her. That she had meant something to him.

And there it was.

Sitting at the outlook, in "their" spot.

A new bench made of oak and iron filigree.

Had he done this?

Or had the park just finally decided it needed a bench here?

She crossed to the bench, ran her hand across the fresh wood. The back of the bench curved along the top rail, and a small plaque was embedded in the wood in the center of the rail.

Reese leaned forward to read it. "In memory of Bud and Dorothy O'Neal: For loving the falls and sharing it with their granddaughter."

A sob burst out as she sank onto the bench, the warmth of the wood surrounding her like an embrace. As if she could actually feel her grandparents here with her.

That was silly. Her grandparents weren't here.

And neither was Wade.

But she swore she could feel her grandparents' spirit, and she drew strength from it, soaking it in like the warm sunshine against her face.

And now she knew.

Wade *did* care about her. She *had* meant something to him.

But was that enough?

It had to be.

She'd wanted to take control of her life and this was her life now. With or without Wade, this new life in Cotton Creek was what she wanted.

Despite the jagged pain in her heart, she was still excited about the opportunity to work at the newspaper. Harry had told her he had a nephew in publishing, and when her book was ready, he would get his nephew to take a look at it.

The possibilities seemed wide open to her, from choosing her own place to live and picking the decorations she wanted. She could wake up in the morning and be excited to go to a job doing something she loved.

She would miss a few of her customers, like the Donaldsons. But she had told them her plans last week, and they'd applauded the idea and promised to drive into the mountains and take her out for coffee to celebrate her new job.

Everything seemed to be working out.

Everything except Wade.

Stop it. Pull yourself together. She'd be okay. Everything was going to be fine.

So why were her hands shaking? And why did she feel like she was going to throw up?

She finally had the life she wanted. She was going to make

this work.

She swiped the back of her hand across her cheek, wiping away the single tear that had leaked from her eye.

Taking a deep breath, she ignored the bone-deep ache in her heart and steeled herself to embrace her new life.

The sun shone down on the water, making rainbows in the air. It was a warm summer day, and she was in the place that her grandparents had loved. That she loved.

Where she had met a man who had filled her life with happiness and tears. With joy and sorrow. With fried food, iced coffee, and a whole lot of crazy fun.

She could do this.

She stood and turned toward the falls.

And he was there.

Her breath stopped, and the fist that had tightened around her heart let loose. "Wade?"

He strode toward her, his steps full of purpose, and he pulled her into his arms. Cupping her neck, he tipped up her face and crushed his lips against hers, taking her mouth with heat and passion.

He pulled her tighter against him and kissed her neck, her shoulder, that spot right below her ear. "I couldn't go. God help me, I couldn't walk away from you."

Wrapping her arms around him, she held on tight, afraid to let go. "You came back."

He looked down at her. "I don't know what the future holds or how this idea of you living in Cotton Creek is going to go, but I don't want to miss the chance to find out."

She gripped his face between her hands and looked him straight in the eye, trying to convey the depths of her feelings. "This isn't all just some experiment to me. I'm not going anywhere. I'm here to stay. This is the life I want. *You* are what I want."

His voice was gruff, hoarse with emotion. "You're what I

want, too. I tried to fight it, tried to tell myself I was better off without you. I tried to drive away. But I couldn't. I want that life with you. I want to wake up every day with your beautiful face on the pillow across from mine. I want to bring you maple donuts and take you dancing. I want to go hiking and fishing and skinny-dipping in the lake with you."

Her heart filled to overflowing.

He was saying everything she longed to hear. Except the most important thing.

His actions of putting in the bench proved he cared about her, but she still needed to hear him say it. "So I *do* mean something to you?"

"Mean something? You mean *everything*. I love you, Reese. And I even love that funny dog of yours."

She laughed. His last comment sealed the deal. That was all she needed to hear.

She pulled his face down and planted a fierce kiss on his lips. "I love you, too, Wade."

He drew her tighter against him and slid his hands under her sweatshirt. A surprised look crossed his face, and he arched an eyebrow. "Are you not wearing a bra?"

She giggled. And it felt good. Everything felt so good now. So right.

Her soul filled with happiness, here in her favorite place, with the man she loved.

She looked into his gorgeous eyes and teased, "I figured the best way to romance a ranger was to get back to nature and *bare* it all."

He grinned. "You figured right."

THE END

Acknowledgments

My thanks always goes first to my husband, Todd, the one who supports me and believes in me. I love and adore you. Thanks for taking this and all journeys with me.

Thanks to my sons, Tyler and Nick, for your love and support. You guys make it all worth it.

Thanks so much to my amazing editor, Allison Collins for your hard work and dedication to making this book happen. And thanks to the whole crew at Entangled Publishing for giving your valuable time and energy to publish this book.

My thanks always goes out to the women that walk this writing journey with me every day. The ones that make me laugh, who encourage and support, who offer great advice and sometimes just listen. Thank you Michelle Major, Lana Williams, Anne Eliot, & Cindi Madsen. XO

Special thanks goes out to Kristin Miller—you have taught me so much—your friendship and plotting help is invaluable.

My biggest thanks goes out to my readers! Thanks for loving my stories and my characters and for continuing to ask for more. I can't wait to share my next story with you.

About the Author

USA TODAY Best-selling author Jennie Marts loves to make readers laugh as she weaves stories filled with love, friendship and intrigue. Reviewers call her books "laugh out loud" funny and full of great characters.

She is living her own happily ever after in the mountains of Colorado with her own Prince Charming. She's addicted to Diet Coke, adores Cheetos, and believes you can't have too many books, shoes, or friends.

Her books include the following series: the Hearts of Montana, the Page Turners, the Bannister Brothers Books, and the Cotton Creek Romances.

Jennie loves to hear from readers. Follow her on Facebook at Jennie Marts Books, or Twitter at @JennieMarts. Visit her at www.jenniemarts.com.

Also by Jennie Marts...

TUCKED AWAY

New Yorker Charlie Ryan hits rock bottom until she inherits a Montana farm called Tucked Away. Now her hands are full of wheat, cows, and one very hot veterinarian. Zack Cooper is wary of this sexy city slicker and her hot-pink cowboy boots. He's been burned once, and knows Charlie might get bored and head back for the bright lights of the big city. Their hearts have been tucked away too long…do they dare risk them for a new love?

HIDDEN AWAY

Her cousin's death leaves restuarant owner Cherry Hill sole guardian of her eight-year-old nephew. To help her keep custody, Taylor Johnson, the man who broke her heart nine years ago, steps in. Sheriff Johnson protects the citizens of Broken Falls, but a fake engagement to the woman he fell for so long ago is going above and beyond. Before long, his pretend feeings turn real for both Cherry and Sam. But Cherry's been hiding a secret from Taylor that could rip this new family apart…

LOVING HER CRAZY
a *Crazy Love* novel by Kira Archer

Iris Clayton is supposed to be on a tropical island. Instead, she's snowbound in Chicago overnight. Good thing there's a hot cowboy to keep her company—a cowboy that can make her tremble with one sultry look from under his well-worn hat. Montana rancher Nash Wallace had no idea roaming the city could be so fun—or illegal. Now he's falling hard and fast. Wanting to spend his life with someone after one night is insane. Except, nothing has ever felt so right, and neither of them wants the night to end...

UNEXPECTEDLY HIS
a *Smart Cupid* novel by Maggie Kelley

Marianne McBride just wanted to prove she's more than a computer geek in a pair of horn-rimmed glasses. How exactly did she find herself hiding in a cake, waiting to sing "Happy Birthday" to Nick Wright, the sexy and arrogant serial-dater she's been crushing on? Nick falls for no woman, but he needs to find the perfect faux fiancée or kiss his key to the executive washroom goodbye. Fortunately, his matchmaker sister has the perfect girl in mind...

LOVING THE ODDS
a *What Happens in Vegas* novella by Stefanie London

Bailey Reuben might be in Las Vegas, but the *last* thing on her mind is sin. She's there to find her jerk of an ex and get her grandfather's watch back. Instead, she meets a sexy stranger with a crazy plan to help her retrieve her family heirloom. With bad boy PR guru Lance Fulton pretending to be her boyfriend, she'll get the watch—*and* revenge. But the hotter their attraction burns, the higher the probability one of them will end up with a broken heart…

A Change of Plans
a *What Happens in Vegas* novella by Robyn Thomas

Sara Greaves has been planning her perfect wedding since she was five. Instead, she's dumped by her fiancé and meets Ethan Munroe—Mr. Dall, Dark, And Anti-Marriage—who bets that she could marry any guy in Vegas and make it work. Only now Ethan has a hangover, a wedding band, and a sexy, gorgeous bride for the next month—who doesn't want to stay married to him. He never planned this, but he can't bring himself to go for the speedy divorce. Has Mr. Anti-Marriage finally met his match?